A few years ago, Detective Jackson Blue made a promise to a teenage street hustler named Tyler. He told him that he would protect him in exchange for information, but in spite of his effort, Tyler ended up dead. Jackson is convinced that his pimp, Manny the Saint, is responsible but has no proof. When a temper problem lands Jackson yet another suspension; Jackson hits the streets in disguise to try and find a lead.

Blake Wellington is a dancer, who hustles on the side, at the club owned by Manny the Saint. He's known Manny since he was a teenager and figures that Manny saved his life. When he is approached on the street one night by a raggedly man with a pocket full of cash, he threatens to pepper spray him. In spite of the money the vagrant is offering, Blake is turned off at the prospect of having sex with him. With the promise that the man will take a shower, Blake reluctantly agrees, having no idea of the surprises that await him.

Covetous Pursuits is a story of one man's quest to find a killer, with a few twists and turns along the way, and some very hot sex that may or may not, turn out to mean much more.

Covetous Pursuits
Copyright © 2018 D.J. Manly
ISBN: 978-1-4874-2363-6
Cover art by Martine Jardin

Published by eXtasy Books Inc or
Devine Destinies, an imprint of eXtasy Books Inc

Look for us online at:
www.eXtasybooks.com or www.devinedestinies.com

# COVETOUS PURSUITS

## BY

## D.J. MANLY

# CHAPTER ONE

There was some commotion going on outside April Grant's door. It was enough to rouse Jackson from the nap he'd been taking. He yawned, stretched a little, and sat upright, waiting. The door flew open. Two women stumbled into the hallway, hands hungrily roving flesh as they ripped at each other's clothes. April propelled the other woman all the way into the apartment, slamming her against the wall, closing the door with her foot.

*You go, girl.* He never knew April had it in her.

Jackson crossed his arms over his tattered khaki jacket and tilted his head. He smiled. All that was missing really was the popcorn.

The two women continued their amorous adventure, oblivious to his presence as they gulped kisses. At one point, Jackson considered clearing his throat or something, but no, this was way too much fun.

April suddenly pushed the woman away, giving her a lecherous grin. "Let's go to the bedroom where I can show you—" Then she stopped.

He surmised that April had spotted him out of the corner of her eye. When her hand went for her gun holster, Jackson jumped to his feet, hands in the air. "Whoa, whoa, you're not going to shoot me, are you, April? They took my gun away, remember?"

The other woman looked from Jackson to April, a baffled expression on her flushed face as she hastily tried to pull her t-shirt down.

"What the hell are you doing here?" April demanded, coming closer. "And what's with the get-up?"

Jackson motioned with his head to the woman who stood frozen a few feet away. "Aren't you going to introduce me to your friend before you interrogate me, Officer?"

April scowled at him. "You know who she is."

She did seem familiar.

The woman stepped forward. "Verity Monk, fifteenth precinct. Who is this guy?" she asked April.

"No one," April snapped.

Jackson laughed. "Thanks."

"Have we met?" the other woman enquired. "Do you need help?"

"What he needs is a damn shrink," April muttered under her breath.

Jackson put a hand on his heart as if she'd wounded him.

"Don't worry, Verity." April sighed. "He's harmless. He's just my partner, Jackson Blue, and he was just leaving."

"Well, I won't intrude any longer," Jackson said. "I'll just—"

"No," Verity Monk said. "I'll go." She gave April a look of longing. "I have an early shift tomorrow anyway. Rain check?"

April walked with her to the door. They spoke quietly for a few minutes then Verity Monk left. April closed the door and turned around, hands on her hips. "What are you doing here, Jackson?"

"You are giving me the ugly face."

"Where the hell have you been? You haven't answered your phone in days."

"Street people don't have phones, usually."

"Street people?" she repeated. "Great. And what's with that horrible beard and those clothes? New fashion statement?"

"I've found him," Jackson told her.

April indicated the open bottle of scotch sitting on the coffee table. "Looks like you found my liquor, too."

Jackson picked up the bottle. "Want some?"

"Am I going to need some?" April demanded.

"Maybe."

"I'll get glasses." April walked to the kitchen cupboards.

"So, really? A cop?" Jackson chuckled.

"Don't give me any grief." April pointed at him. She came back with the glasses. "You used to live with a cop."

Jackson poured the liquor into the glasses. "Yeah, and you remember how that turned out."

"It's just sex," she said, plopping on the sofa and tossing back the liquor.

"Heard that one before. Said it a few times myself, then you end up making them breakfast."

She eyed him. "Never mind my sex life, or, thanks to you, lack thereof."

"Can't blame all of it on me." He grinned.

"So, you found him, The Milker, or whatever it is he's called."

Jackson grinned. "The Drain, but I suppose The Milker would work, too."

"So, that's why you've forgotten what a razor and," she sniffed the air, "a shower is for?"

"More or less." Jackson swallowed some of the scotch. It was going down far too easily lately. Ever since he'd got suspended, his drinking had doubled.

"So, wait until you're reinstated and haul his ass in. Is he still working the streets?" April asked.

"I think he's still turning tricks but I'm not so sure he's doing it on the street corner. He works as an erotic dancer."

"A little old, isn't he?"

"He looks super young for his age. The johns probably

think he's fifteen or so, but he's at least nineteen. I know he has a special relationship with Manny the Saint. I've watched them together. Manny owns the dive where this guy dances. From what I've been able to find out, when Manny went underground, after Tyler was murdered, he took The Drain with him."

"Boyfriend?" April asked as she held out her glass for a refill

"Let's say, number one boy. I don't think you could apply the label of boyfriend." Jackson refilled her glass.

"So, Manny took this kid with him to keep him quiet about Tyler's murder? Why didn't he just kill him?"

"Probably would have drawn too much attention, raised red flags."

"Um, you're right. This Drain, he could have seen something."

"For sure, he knows more about Manny than anyone else who might have been around at that time. The ones we could track down were all questioned after Tyler's murder. No one was talking."

"So, what are you going to do, Jackson?" She leaned forward. "You got to be careful. You're on suspension. Your hearing is coming up soon. You got to keep out of trouble until then."

Jackson laughed. "Who you talking to? Me in trouble?"

She rolled her eyes. "So, what's your plan?"

"I'm going to pick him up, find out if he really is The Drain." Jackson lifted an eyebrow a few times.

She laughed. "Right. Be damn good and sure he's not a minor. That's all you need now, a morals charge."

"He's not a minor. He wasn't sucking dick at eight."

"Speaking of cock suckers," April said, meeting his gaze. "Ever hear from Rob?"

"Nope, and I don't care to. Someone told me he was

working in Boston. That's all I know. Don't really give a shit."

She took his hand. "Listen to me. If this doesn't work out, if this guy doesn't help you find the proof you need that Manny murdered Tyler, promise me you'll drop it."

Jackson finished his liquor. He couldn't make a promise like that.

"Jackson," April insisted. "What happened to Tyler wasn't your fault."

He swallowed. "I gotta go." He got to his feet. "I need to borrow some money for the subway." He held out his hand.

"You haven't paid me back for the money you borrowed last time," she accused, grabbing her wallet off the coffee table. "And where is your car?"

"I left it in a parking lot near Times Square," Jackson told her.

She handed him the money. "You look so bizarre, scary with that big beard."

He grinned and pulled his hoodie over his head. "Boo."

"Where have you been sleeping?"

"Where the homeless sleep," he said.

"You really slept in a—" April's eyes widened.

"You want to learn things on the streets, you gotta live on 'em. How about a kiss?" He made a show of pursing his lips and making a noise like a guppy next to her cheek.

She pushed him away. "Get out of here," she said, "or I will shoot you. And you owe me almost a hundred bucks now."

Jackson headed to the door. "If we both weren't so queer, you could take it out in trade, especially since you've only got the trusty old vibrator tonight." He glanced back to see a look of outrage on her face. "I know how much you like cops, April, but I can't help you out there." He winked and walked out.

Something was thrown at the door as he walked away. He laughed all the way down the stairs.

When Jackson got outside April's building, he braced himself for the blast of frigid air he knew would greet him. He was hoping that tonight would be the night he'd make contact. His suspension from the force wouldn't last forever. This was the ideal time to do this. He was going to get a slap on the wrist and sent back to that therapist who liked to use fancy words like, *Anger Management* and *Post Traumatic Stress Syndrome.* Yes, damn it, he was angry. And even now as he made his way to the nearest subway station, rage clawed at his insides, as fresh as ever. And no, it wasn't because, as the shrink told him, he'd modeled off his father. Dad had also been a cop. He'd been a mean bastard, that was no lie. His father had come home and taken all the frustrations out on his wife and children. It was true Jackson had gotten his temper from the old man, and lately the drinking, but he wasn't his father. Dad had died shortly after Jackson had graduated from the academy. He'd only been retired for two years. He'd spent his time with retired policemen, reminiscing about the job and making love to the bottle. A few months after his father had retired, Jackson left home. That's when his mother had taken his sister and left. Without Jackson, no one would be around to protect them, a role that had been thrust upon him since puberty. Unfortunately, it was too late to save his sister, Marilyn, who was already hitting the bottle pretty hard at fourteen. She'd been in and out of rehab, and Jackson had tried to help her many times, but she couldn't stay sober. It broke his heart, but he'd given up. Last he'd heard, she was living with yet another bum, living on food stamps.

The academy had saved him from himself. And it was the one thing he and the old man had in common, their love for the job. The only time Richard Blue had ever said he was proud of him was the day Jackson showed up in his hospital room in uniform. The old man had never approved of anything Jackson did, except for becoming a cop. Jackson had never told him he was gay. The last thing he'd said to Jackson was, "Finally, you did something right." His funeral was attended by a sea of cops who worshipped him and a family who didn't know how to grieve a man who'd given them nothing but grief.

Jackson had devoted himself to police work from his first day on the job. When he'd met April Burns, she'd been a detective for three years, something he definitely aspired to. That was almost seven years ago.

Jackson quickly realized that April was brilliant. She was the youngest female detective on the force, only twenty-six. Jackson did all he could to impress her. When April had chosen him for an undercover operation about a year after he'd joined the force, he was really excited. She'd praised his work and asked him to do other undercover work. When he had run into April at the Pride Parade that summer, this sealed their bond, and they had become friends. They were the only two cops in their division who'd marched in the parade with the NYPD. Three years later, thanks to April's encouragement, Jackson made detective, and they became partners.

That's when Rob Rosetti had come on the scene, a transfer from another division where things were not going well. He was in his early forties, handsome, intelligent, and all about the job. Jackson had fallen for him like a ton of bricks, and eventually, it became apparent that Rob felt the same. They quickly became lovers, keeping their affair on the low brow.

Jackson put Rob out of his mind as he got onto the subway, finding a seat in the corner. He was grateful to be out of the cold. No one really looked at him. The irony, he'd discovered, of being a vagrant, was that although you were readily identifiable as a street person, people pretended not to see you. He closed his eyes. He was tired. There was a good half-hour ride to the 42nd Street terminal, so he'd take another quick nap. He hadn't slept well in the shelters, nor in his car, but if he could make contact tonight, it would be all worth it.

The minute he'd been handed the suspension three weeks ago, he'd decided it was time to give his pursuit of Manny the Saint another try. He knew Manny had resurfaced, like a rat coming out of hiding when it thought no one was look-ing. Manny had collected a new stable of boys and girls and was busy hanging out with his friends from the mob at the strip clubs. Jackson watched Manny at every opportunity, but the last thing he wanted was the creep to discover Jack-son's surveillance. Like the rat he was, Manny would squirm back into some hole somewhere if he felt cornered.

Every time Jackson closed his eyes lately, he saw Tyler. So fragile, with his innocent face and pale blond hair. April had told him not to blame himself for his murder, but how could he do otherwise? He'd been blind, manipulated by Rob, who'd told him nothing would happen to Tyler. Jackson should have followed his instincts, but at that time Rob was his everything. But Rob had never really cared about Tyler. He'd just wanted to use him to get to Anthony Adele, some low-grade mobster, who'd ended up at the bottom of the Hudson anyway.

Jackson had been one of the detectives on Rob's team. They were going to shake down Manny Celino, better known on the streets as Manny the Saint, a pimp, a drug dealer, who was protected by the mob. Celino was close to someone in one of the leading crime families—someone from his family had intermarried, no one really knew how it worked. Manny would be easy to nab, then Rob figured they could offer him a deal, to get Adele. In the crossfires was Tyler, a fourteen-year-old boy Manny had working for him on the streets. Rob told Jackson to befriend Tyler, pretend to be a john, see if he could get some information on Manny. Tyler wanted off the streets. Rob wanted to keep him on the streets as an informant.

"You will protect me, won't you, Jack?" Tyler looked up at him. "He'll kill me if he knows I'm talking to the cops."

"I won't let anything happen to you, Tyler," Jackson promised him.

Tears stung Jackson's eyes now. He opened them, blinking the tears away. He swallowed hard. He was sure Manny had murdered Tyler, even left a note, reminding Jackson that he'd lied to Tyler, hadn't protected him after all. After that, Jackson's life seemed to fall apart. He left Rob, blaming him for not doing enough to protect the boy. Rob put in for another transfer. All Jackson had left was the job, April, and his thirst for vengeance.

Manny was still walking around out there. He'd run scared after Tyler's death. Jackson had tracked him down, threatened his life, put him in the hospital. It had led to his first suspension. Manny had laughed in his face at the murder accusation, telling Jackson to *prove it*. Twenty-four hours later, Jackson was arrested for assault. Then, the creep got himself lawyered up. Jackson got suspended, almost lost his badge. Luckily the case was dropped when Manny didn't show up in court. He'd skipped town. The guy was a little worm, a murderous piece of shit. And Jackson would never give up trying to avenge Tyler's death, even if it meant his badge.

"I may have not been there to protect you, Tyler," Jackson vowed under his breath as he got off the subway, "but I won't rest until that prick is either behind bars for your murder, or in the ground."

Jackson raised the hoodie over his head and rubbed the

beard. He wasn't used to having a beard that thick. It was beginning to itch. As soon as he made contact and got this guy back to his place, he was shaving it off.

Jackson had learned a lot about The Drain in the two weeks he'd been out on the streets, everything but his real name. On most nights, he danced in a creepy dive just off Broadway called The Ball and Chain. It was primarily a gay bar for a ragtag bunch of weirdos who wore fake leather and acted like they were all auditioning for some S and M show. The bar said Ladies Welcome, but Jackson didn't see ladies in there. Manny had bought the bar, and most nights could be seen there playing manager and hosting a bunch of *wise guys*.

The Drain was a creature of habit. He came out of there just before closing. Then he'd hail a cab. He probably had a *date* somewhere. Tight jeans, short leather jacket—a real one—thick curly brown hair and the face of a teenager, The Drain might not have been walking the streets anymore, but word had it that he was still in high demand, and his services didn't come cheap.

Jackson stomped his feet and fingered the money in his pocket. His car was a block away. He couldn't go inside the club to wait because the last time he'd ventured in there, the bouncer had asked him to leave. Manny had been there at a table up front, so Jackson had left right away, not wanting to draw attention to himself. But he'd seen him dance, the man who looked like a boy. He was popular—the patrons shouted and cheered when he came on stage. What made a grown man want to have sex with a boy, a child? He thought of Tyler. He'd been a baby, and how those johns used and abused him ... Was it control, power, a lack of confidence in a man's own sexual abilities that compelled him to want a boy instead of a man? Whatever it was, it was something Jackson would never understand.

10

Yes, this one may look like a boy, but he was no boy. He was a grown man who knew exactly how to seduce from that stage, how to entice one to pull out those bills. His body was smooth and well-muscled, and he danced naked without any inhibitions, pushing his hips in and out in a way that left no room for misinterpretation. Jackson found it hard to look away. As a gay man, it was a challenge not to feel turned on. His mouth went a little dry, and his imagination ignited. He saw himself up there with him on that stage, grabbing his hips, stabbing that gorgeous, round ass with his erect cock. The sound of their fucking, hard and fast, materialized in his head, drowning out the actual music that was playing in the club. He wondered if he wasn't the same as all the others, titillated by his youthful appearance, making you want to possess and dominate him. That's when someone's hand landed on his arm, telling him to leave.

Jackson had found himself looking at the bouncer, a big guy, who was ready to toss him out the door. "We don't accept bums in here."

"I'll go," he'd told him.

The cold wind was howling around him now, just like it had the night he'd been thrown out of the club. Ice pellets this time. Jackson moved closer to the wall in the alley, keeping the club in view. His beard was covered with frost. He knew he must look like some Neanderthal who'd just been dug out of a block of ice. The cold was making him sleepy. He closed his eyes a few times then stamped feet he could no longer feel. He thought about running up the street to get his car, but he was afraid to miss him. There was no place to park anyway.

*Come on. Please be alone.*

Then The Drain came out of that dance bar. He paused at the entrance, chatting with a few people before calling out goodnight. They were shutting the lights off at the club.

*Come on. Come on.*

11

Finally, there was another chorus of goodnights. The Drain was walking down the street in his direction. Jackson watched him in disbelief. On a night like tonight, only tight leather pants and a short black leather jacket covered him. His boots were merely decorative and didn't look like anything you'd wear in deep snow. There was no hat or gloves. Obviously, the guy was dressed to attract attention. It was a wonder he didn't freeze to death in the process.

Jackson stepped out of the shadows.

He'd startled him. The Drain took a step back. "Listen," he said, pointing at him, appearing to be more annoyed than scared. "I have pepper spray in my pocket, and no money on me. So, don't think you're going to mug me, old man."

*Old man?* Jackson wanted to laugh. Maybe he did look like an old man. "You won't need the pepper spray," Jackson told him. "I have ten, one hundred dollar bills here." He showed him the roll of money he had clenched in his fist. "What can I get for that?"

His eyes widened. "What's a homeless person doing with a thousand dollars?"

"I'm not homeless. I have a place, a car. Want to come with me or not? I doubt you'll get a better offer tonight. The snow is starting to come down pretty heavy again. So, what can I get for a grand?"

"Ah, I don't know." He gave Jackson an up-and-down appraisal and shook his head. "I don't think so. You been in the war or something? I'm usually kind to veterans but I do have my limits."

Damn. He didn't think a hustler would be so put off by appearances that he'd turn down that much cash. The disguise had mostly been for Manny's benefit. Now he wished he'd cleaned up before approaching him. "Ah, yeah," he said when he realized The Drain hadn't run away. "A war. I'm in a war." *Yes, and there is only one soldier on each side of it.*

"I really do need something tonight. I'm not fussy."

"One thousand dollars, huh?" He eyed the money. "Is it real?"

"Yeah." Jackson met his eyes. "It's real."

"I don't kiss."

Jackson shrugged. "Okay. You fuck and suck, right?"

"Sure," he said. "That's fine, but no bondage, weird shit, or peeing, pooping on me, that kind of thing. And could you take a shower or something before? I don't want your cooties."

"Not a problem. Let's go. I'm freezing my ass off here."

"Is the car far away?" The Drain asked, hurrying to catch up with him. He slipped a few times but didn't fall.

"A block. What's your name?" Jackson started up the street, The Drain at his heels.

"Just call me B."

"B it is," Jackson said. His car was in the parking lot, and it was covered with snow. "Get in," he told B, opening the door with his remote. "I'll clean her off."

There was no hesitation. The Drain opened the passenger side and got in, closing the door after him. Jackson began to clear the snow away. He glanced at his passenger once to see him texting someone. He'd love to get hold of that phone.

When the windshield and the roof was cleared of snow, Jackson got behind the wheel. B had put his phone away. Jackson started the engine and the wipers. The snow was more like freezing rain now. What a mess!

"Dodge Challengers are pricy, aren't they?" B spoke up as Jackson pulled out of the parking lot and onto the street. "This is a what? Twenty-fourteen?"

"You know your cars," Jackson said, scratching his beard. *God, I have to get rid of this.*

"So, if you're not a street person, what do you do for a living? Not everyone can spend a grand on a hustler. You must be pretty desperate. I can kinda see why. No one is going to have sex with you for free, right?"

Jackson glanced at him. "For a hustler, you're don't have much of a way with words. Are you trying to make me feel bad?"

"I call them as I see 'em." He shrugged. "Some people are born with looks, and others, well, are just sad."

"Charming." Jackson stopped at the traffic light.

"I cancelled a date tonight for you," he pointed out. "It was only a blow job. Doesn't pay enough to keep me in the lifestyle of which I'm accustomed." He chuckled, clearly expecting a reaction.

"So, how do you cancel a blow job? Is it like cancelling a dentist's appointment? You keep your clients on speed dial? One for blow job, two for a screw?"

"Are you being sarcastic?"

Jackson grinned and hit the gas.

"You know, you're a good driver," B pointed out, "but you drive way too fast. If I was a cop, I'd give you a ticket."

"Good thing you're not a cop then."

"I've met some bad eggs, fucking cops. They'd be better off arresting killers and shit, instead of going off on poor people trying to make a living."

"Agreed."

"You ever spend a night in jail?" he asked.

"Yeah, I have," Jackson admitted.

"What did you do, scare the shit out of someone?"

Jackson glanced at him. "I beat a guy to within a few inches of his life."

"Let me out of this car," B bellowed

Jackson put a hand on his arm. "Relax, I'm not going to beat you. I didn't pick you up for that."

"Good." He seemed to breathe easier. "You're not the usual type of john."

"What is a usual type of john?"

"Some middle-aged married guy. Old farts like you are rare."

Jackson turned the corner which led to his basement apartment. "How old do you think I am?"

"I don't know, ah . . . fifty?"

Jackson laughed out loud. Either this guy was a horrible judge of age or Jackson had gone overboard with the beard. He suspected it was a little of both. He was only wrong by about twenty-three years. Anyway, it didn't matter. He felt fifty right now. But finally, he had him, the only link to Manny the Saint. He couldn't fuck this up. This was his last chance to nail Manny for Tyler's murder.

"So, you going to tell me?" B probed. "I'm a professional, you know. Old dudes can't get it up as fast, and it takes longer to come. I can help you with that."

"Good to know." Jackson smiled.

"I once did a guy who was over seventy."

"And how did that work out?" Jackson kept his focus on the road, what he could see of it.

"He went to sleep in the middle of it. I thought he was dead."

Jackson widened his eyes. "Was he?"

"He kind of gasped, you know, and then his eyes closed. I didn't even get him half erect."

"What happened?"

"I woke him up and gave him his money back."

"Ah, what a prince."

"Sarcasm again?" B muttered.

"We're here," Jackson said, turning into the driveway and parking in his spot. He lived in the basement of a duplex. It was a nice place, one bedroom, bathroom, large living room with galley kitchen. There was even an electric fireplace in the living room where he had his enormous, flat-screen television and L-shaped sofa.

They got out of the car, and Jackson locked up. "Are you hungry?" he asked him, leading him to door. The path had been shoveled by Dany already, the owner who lived above him. He'd even put down some sand. Still, this guy was slipping all over the place.

"Yeah, I could eat," B said.

"I'll order pizza?"

"Pesto shrimp," he suggested. "Unless you don't like it."

"No, that's cool," Jackson said as he opened the door with his key and switched on the light. "You can leave your boots there on the carpet," Jackson instructed, pulling off his own. Damn. It was good to be home. He needed to get rid of this beard and take a shower, pronto. Maybe B would open up a little more. He really did seem put off by him.

"This is nice," B said, sitting on the sofa. He glanced over at the weights in the corner. "Who works out here, your son?"

"My alter ego," Jackson told him.

Jackson walked over and turned on the electric fireplace then grabbed his phone off the counter. He'd left it plugged in. He had twenty-seven voice mail messages and sixteen missed calls, mostly from work. He didn't see anything from Internal Affairs yet. He pressed speed dial for his favorite pizza place and waited.

"Sophie, it's Jackson," he said into the receiver. "Is it too bad out there for you guys to deliver an extra-large pesto shrimp?"

"Nope, for you, my darling, anything," she said. "Something else?"

"A big bottle of cola."

"Okay, half hour."

"Thanks." He hung up.

B had taken off his coat, leaving only a t-shirt. "That looks like the real thing," he said, referring to the fireplace.

Jackson nodded. "Yeah, it does. Throws a lot of heat." He studied him a moment. B had pulled a blanket up over him. "Tell me something."

"Okay." He looked at him, folding his feet up under him on the sofa.

"How can you walk around dressed the way you do when it's twenty-seven degrees outside?"

"You must suffer to be attractive, darling." He laughed, making an exaggerated motion with his hand.

He looked so young at that moment, Jackson was taken aback. "How old are you?"

"How old do you want me to be?" He winked.

"Seriously?"

"I'm nineteen on the birth certificate, but on the streets, fourteen, sometimes fifteen."

"You won't be able to pull that off forever," Jackson commented.

"I have a backup plan." He seemed sleepy. "Can you put on some music?"

"Okay. What do you want to listen to?" Jackson asked him.

"Doesn't matter."

Jackson switched on the radio. "Classic rock channel?"

"Yeah, that's nice."

"I'll be about twenty minutes. I'm trusting you not to run off with the pizza money. Can you answer the door when they come?"

"I'm not a thief," he protested. "Besides, its cozy here. I am not venturing back out there tonight. A grand will get you me, until morning."

Jackson nodded and headed for the bathroom. "The money's on the counter."

In the bathroom, Jackson peeked in the mirror and even scared himself. He did look like a homeless person—and old. The beard was scraggly, like a hornet's nest. Jackson took out a pair of scissors and started hacking off chunks of beard. He plugged in his electric razor and moved it over his jaw, eventually getting that perfect, five o'clock shadow back. He stripped off his clothes and got into the shower. Damn, it felt good.

# CHAPTER TWO

Blake had turned off his cellphone. In spite of the fact that the guy was old and unattractive, he seemed normal enough. It was warm here with the artificial flames glowing in the fireplace. He put the blanket over him and closed his eyes while some Bon Jovi song played on the radio. This was a great trick, considering he was getting paid more than his usual, and he was even going to be fed. He was almost asleep when the doorbell rang.

"Ah, whatever your name is . . . ah . . . the pizza is here." There was no answer, so Blake got off the sofa and went to the door. The guy shivered. "How much?"

The guy checked the bill, handing Blake a bottle of cola. "Thirty-three twenty- eight, and the tip?"

Blake put down the soft drink and took the two twenties that were on the counter. "Right." Blake grinned. "Okay, here you go." He handed him the two twenties and took the pizza. "Keep the change."

"Thanks, buddy," he said.

Blake closed the door and put the pizza on the counter. He wandered down the hallway. "Hey, ah, the pizza is here."

The bathroom door opened. This tall, dark-haired god stood there, wearing only a pair of gray sweatpants, his skin glistening from a shower.

*Yum.* "Hey," Blake said, letting his gaze run the length of him. All those muscles. He was tall, black hair a little long and wild, but he could live with that. Sexy shadow on his jaw, full lips. Okay, he wanted some. Where was the old guy?

"Looking for something?" the god asked.

"Ah, what happened to the . . . other man, your father? Who . . . are you again?" Blake actually licked his lips, eyeing those muscular pectorals.

"I am the old guy," he said, meeting Blake's gaze.

Blue eyes, black hair, damn.

"Did the pizza come?" he asked.

"You're not fifty," Blake accused, shaking his head. "You are not that old guy. And you're hot as hell."

Jackson grinned. "Thank you. Start on the pizza. I was just going to find a t-shirt."

"Don't bother putting a shirt on for me," he said, gaze settling on his chest. "Did I just win the lottery?"

"Do you play the lottery?" he asked.

"I think I'm going to start."

"Why don't you get some plates and cutlery out of the cupboard so we can eat? I'll join you in a minute."

Blake watched the man walk off into the bedroom. Oh God, he had a great ass, too, a round bubble ass that even the sweatpants couldn't hide. Now he was confused. Blake took out the plates and the forks and poured some cola into glasses.

The hunk appeared shortly after, wearing a light-blue t-shirt. It was tight across the chest and arms, which was a visual treat. Now, if he was hung, too, Blake was going to lay at the man's feet.

"Found everything?" He put a piece of pizza on a plate and grabbed a glass.

Blake did the same and came to sit beside him on the sofa. "Can you please tell me why a man that is as hot as you are, would hide under that ugly beard? I'm confused. What's going on? Did you really bring me here for sex?"

"No," he said.

"That's disappointing," Blake said. "Then what am I doing here? Was that money you showed me real?"

"Yes. I'm going to give you the money," he said, taking a bite out of his pizza.

Blake did the same, realizing how hungry he was. "A guy like you doesn't pay for sex."

He sat back against the sofa. "I need your help."

Blake took another bite of pizza and then put the plate down on the coffee table. "To do what?"

"You promise you'll stay until morning even if you don't like what I have to say?"

He shrugged. "Okay."

"Do you remember a boy called Tyler Kowal?"

Blake sucked in some breath. He didn't want to think about Tyler. He stiffened. "How do you know him?"

"I asked you if you knew him."

"No, never heard of him," Blake said, shaking his head. "What are you, a cop?" He jumped to his feet. "Is that why you brought me here, to ask me questions? I don't know anything. I didn't see anything. Okay?" He rushed over to where his boots were.

The man was at the door, blocking his path. "I can't let you go until you tell me if you knew him or not. You've been one of Manny's boys for some time now. You were around when Tyler was killed."

Blake threw his boot down on the floor. "I didn't know him well. I might have seen him once or twice. Now, let it go."

"I can't let it go," the man said.

Blake studied him a moment. Then he gasped. "You're Jackson Blue. You're the cop Tyler talked about all the damn time."

"So, you did know him." The cop folded his arms across

his chest.

"He told me you were beautiful. He said he loved you, that one day he'd marry you." Blake shook his head. "You promised to protect him. You used him and threw him away. That's what cops do. Did you fuck him, too?"

The cop's expression hardened. "No, I didn't fuck him. He was a kid. What kind of a man do you think I am?" There was fury in those blue eyes. "And I didn't use him then throw him away. I tried to help him. He wanted off the streets. Manny wouldn't let go of him. Manny killed Tyler when he found out he was talking to the cops."

Blake walked over and sank down onto the sofa. He put his face in his hands. After he'd composed himself, he glanced up again. "Manny isn't a good man, I know that, but he always looked after me. And I'm not his boy anymore. That's over."

"He owns the club you work at."

"I know, but he doesn't own me."

"You think."

"Listen, I don't give a damn what you believe."

"Do you give a damn about Tyler?"

"I remember he was having problems with Tyler. Tyler told me once about you. That's all I know. And Manny may be a pimp, but I've never seen him lay a hand on his boys."

"His merchandise, you mean."

Blake narrowed his eyes. "I've never been his possession."

"He supplies your drugs, right?"

"I'm clean, have been for three years. I don't touch the stuff anymore," Blake said.

"Do you remember the night Tyler was killed or not?"

He shrugged. "Not really."

"Where were you that night? Where was Manny? Why did Manny drop the assault charges against me and take off suddenly? You went with him, didn't you?"

"He took me with him," Blake corrected him. "I didn't want to stay out there on the streets unprotected."

"Are you saying you had a choice?"

Blake wasn't sure of the answer. "Now, we do a lot of stuff through the internet. It's safer, you know? And I don't need his protection."

"Fine. Where did you go? We know it was somewhere in Italy."

"A rural village, outside Rome. It was a farm, Manny's cousins or something. The town was ah . . . Viterbo."

"Okay, good. Now try to remember where Manny was the night Tyler died."

"No. I'm not going to try and remember anything." He wanted out of here now.

"Listen," the man said, "don't you care that he murdered Tyler?"

"Allegedly murdered. It can't be proven. And I know where my loyalties are, and it's not with cops like you."

"I'm not a cop. I've been suspended from the force."

"Why?" Blake eyed him. "You kill someone?"

"No. I lost my temper with a suspect. I have to go to anger management." His mouth twisted as he said it.

Blake actually laughed. "You sound all excited about it."

"Thrilled. I know the routine. Isn't the first time."

"A real bad boy, eh? Listen," Blake glanced at him as the man sat next to him, "Jackson? Can I call you that?"

"Sure, if you want to."

Blake moved closer. "You are gay, right? I mean, you are just too damn gorgeous to be straight."

"I could be." He met his gaze.

Blake put a hand on his thigh. "Are you hung? Can I see it? I might just cry tears of joy if you are, because you got everything else, including killer blue eyes."

Jackson pushed his hand off his thigh. "Knock it off."

He didn't mean it. Blake could tell by the way his chest was heaving. He wanted it. "Why is there no guy waiting with bated breath in your bed every night, masturbating as they fantasize about getting fucked by your big, juicy cock?" Blake put his hand back on Jackson's thigh.

This time his hand stayed put. Blake watched Jackson bite lightly into his bottom lip then let his tongue moisten the spot. His breathing got a bit faster. Blake moved his hand to the top of Jackson's waistband. He dipped his fingers in, pulling the sweatpants down and lifting out what already was an erect cock. He let it rest out of the pants, as if on display. Damn. It was big. Almost seven inches. What he could do with that.

Blake ran his fingers over Jackson's shaft, moving them lightly over the helmet-shaped head. This wasn't a job tonight, this was going to be pure pleasure. "It's big," Blake said, reaching up one hand and caressing the thick, dark unruly hair that had fallen across his forehead. "Do you know what they call me, Jackson?" he whispered, circling the head of his cock again with his fingers.

Jackson nodded. "Yes, I know. The Drain."

"My reputation precedes me." He looked up at him with a smile. "When I have something this beautiful to work with, well, damn it, first I'm going to suck you dry then get you hard again so that you can fuck me so deep I'm going to taste your come in my mouth." Blake wrapped his fist around Jackson's shaft, pulling a little. "Baby." He slunk down onto the floor between Jackson's knees and gave a strong tug on the pants. Jackson lifted up some, and Blake yanked them off and tossed them away.

Naked, Jackson Blue was a masterpiece of hard sinew, muscle, and beautiful bronze skin. Blake licked the underside of his scrotum. Jackson moaned softly in his throat before one of his hands landed in Blake's hair.

Blake kept licking then sucking with his lips until he swallowed the head of Jackson's cock. Deep-throating him would be somewhat of a challenge, but he was up for it. He was hard himself, something that didn't usually happen this easily with a john. He was thinking about what it would feel like to have Jackson's cock inside him, and it was turning him on big time.

The more he fantasized about being fucked by Jackson, the more enthusiastic he became with his cock sucking. Blake considered it an artform. He hadn't got this reputation for nothing. He actually enjoyed it most of the time, but this, he was really getting off on.

As he took Jackson's cock deeper into his throat, making sure his gag reflex was turned off, he let his hand slide up one of Jackson's thighs. God, the man was buff. Too bad he was a damn cop with too many questions.

Positioning his head, pushing Jackson's thighs wider, Blake opened up his throat. He had a long throat, which really helped to take more cock than most could. Jackson's shaft was thick, and swallowing wasn't easy, but his tutelage was having its desired effect. Jackson was coming and how.

The come flowed into his mouth as Jackson's body convulsed. He was quiet when he came, just a few low sounds of pleasure emanating from his chest. Blake expected that. He could always predict what kind of comer they were beforehand. Big, strong men like Jackson weren't screamers.

Blake backed off, watching as Jackson's chest heaved. He ran a hand across his mouth. Um. He tasted good. Jackson laid a hand on his own chest, leaning back against the sofa, trying to regain his composure.

"You're beautiful when you're out of control," Blake told him, placing his hands on his thighs again and coming up between his knees.

"Not always," Jackson told him.

"Now, take me to bed and fuck me." He reached for Jackson's cock again.

Jackson grabbed Blake's hand and pushed it away. "No," he said. "That was a nice little distraction tactic you pulled, but fucking isn't going to happen." He met Blake's gaze.

Blake got to his feet when Jackson went to stand. "So, that thousand dollars you showed me was bullshit?"

"No, the grand is yours." Jackson reached for the sweatpants and pulled them on.

"That was one expensive blow job," Blake muttered. He reached out and ran a hand over one of Jackson's biceps. Jackson paused. "Why won't you fuck me?"

"Shouldn't that be my line, since I'm paying? It's free money, what's your problem?"

Blake fell quiet. His problem was, he really wanted to fuck this guy. Who in the hell wouldn't? Why was he alone? Why was he throwing around all that money, just to ask a few questions about something that happened ages ago?

"I'm going to clean up," Jackson said, "hit the bed. Listen." He shrugged. "Stay until morning. The sofa is comfortable to sleep on. I'll drive you wherever tomorrow."

Blake nodded. "Okay." He shrugged. "If that's what you want."

"The money is on the counter under the fruit bowl," Jackson said.

"The one with no fruit in it," Blake muttered to himself.

"Goodnight," Jackson said, walking down the hallway.

The bedroom door closed.

Sure enough, the money was there under the empty bowl. Blake grabbed another piece of the pizza, now cold, and bit into it. He sat on the sofa, eating the pizza and thinking about what Jackson had said. Did Manny kill Tyler? Where was he the night Tyler died? It seemed a lifetime ago. Blake had always admired Tyler. He was feisty. He was always mouthing off. You wouldn't think of it to look at him, so delicate, like a china doll someone had broken and put back together again. Blake never knew him too well. Manny didn't encourage the boys to be too friendly with one another. He wanted them to compete, make more and more money. It was the nature of the game. All he knew was that Manny had never been cruel to him. And after Tyler had died, he'd been even nicer, buying him stuff, giving him more and more time off. When they'd left the city for Italy that year, he hadn't had to work at all.

"You're not just my boy," Manny had told him, "we're friends, like brothers."

Blake had never had a brother. In fact, he'd never had anybody. He was on the streets, off and on, at twelve, going from one foster home to another. Then Manny had found him and become his family. He fed him, put a roof over his head, saving him from the streets, protecting him from anyone who would hurt him. No, it wasn't perfect, and Blake knew it was time to leave him. They'd discussed it. Manny said he'd help him if he wanted to go to night school. He owed Manny a lot, but Manny didn't own him.

It was hard to sleep on that sofa. These were his working hours, and the fact that one of the hottest men he'd ever set eyes on was just down the hall wasn't helping at all.

After twenty minutes of tossing and turning, Blake had decided. He was going to take the money, hail a cab, and get out of here. He wasn't sure what made him go down the hallway to take a last peek at him, but he couldn't resist. It wasn't every day you saw a guy who looked that damn good.

Blake slowly opened the bedroom door. The steam of light from the hallway illuminated the figure on the bed, his bare chest rising and falling in a gentle sleep. His head was turned to the side, the sheet resting at his waist.

Blake crept into the room. He almost tripped on something then glanced down to discover the sweatpants Jackson had had on, in a heap on the floor. Oh, he was naked. Blake was tempted to lift the sheet, touch him again, but decided against it. Instead, he leaned down and lightly kissed his forehead. "Sleep well, sweet prince," he whispered.

A hand shot out and gripped his wrist. He froze in his tracks at the sound of Jackson's deep voice. "Thought you didn't kiss?"

Blake smirked. "It wasn't exactly a kiss," he said, trying to pull his hand away.

"Wait, wait," Jackson said, holding tight. He sat up a little in bed. "Where do you think you're going?"

"Why should I stay? You don't want to fuck me."

"I never said I didn't *want to* fuck you." Jackson answered softly.

Blake looked down into those blue eyes. "Okay," he said softly. "What are you waiting for?"

"It's not going to happen," Jackson said, letting his wrist go. "I think I made it clear. I didn't bring you here for that."

"Yet you let me give you a blow job." Blake raised an eyebrow, his mouth twisting.

"You kind of ambushed me there," Jackson accused.

"You're twice my size. I really doubt anyone could blow you without your consent."

Jackson rubbed his eyes. "Okay, fine. I never said I was an angel. Anyway, you'll stay until tomorrow if you want the money."

"Why?" Blake shook his head. "You think I'll tell you all the stuff you want to hear when the sun comes up?"

"Maybe I just want to take you to breakfast." He tossed that out there with a wry grin.

"Right. You are goddamned weird, you know that? Have

you ever been institutionalized?" Blake shook his head in disbelief.

"No, but I probably should have been," he said.

"Fine, I'll sleep on the damn sofa. No one would believe this if I told them."

"Your ego will survive it," he said.

"Is it because I'm not your type?"

"I don't have a type," Jackson replied.

"If you did?" Blake watched his expression.

"Before I make you my damn type, I'd have to know your name. And with a face like a boy and an ass that I'd want to plunder every damn night, what's not to like?"

"But?" Blake said, then held his breath.

"But?" Jackson shook his head. "Soon, I will be a cop again, and you're a hustler with the reputation of being able to suck more dick than a Yankee pitches baseballs."

"That's an advantage, no?"

"Depending how you look at it. Oh, and did I mention that you're connected to the man I detest most on the face of this earth? Do you really think we should be hooking up?"

Blake walked to the door. "Blake," he said at the door. "My name is Blake."

"That's a start."

"Enough to get me into that bed? Just to sleep, mind you."

"Right," Jackson said. "That's what we'd be doing in this bed, Blake, sleeping."

"Can't control yourself, Officer?" Blake leaned on the door. "No self-control?"

"If I'd had any self-control, you wouldn't have been sucking my dick a while ago," he replied dryly.

"Touché."

"See you in the morning," he said gruffly, snuggling back into the pillow. He pulled the sheet over him and turned over on his side.

Back in the living room, Blake switched off the lamp and put his head on the pillow. He watched the flames jumping in the fireplace, and his eyes grew heavy.

It was the smell of coffee that propelled his eyes open again. Blake lifted his head. Jackson Blue stood at the counter. His hair was damp from the shower. In a pair of rather battered jeans and a navy t-shirt, he appeared to be deep in thought as he sipped his coffee. That delinquent tuft of hair of his had fallen over his brow again. It was just too damn sweet. Why did he have to be a cop? And why couldn't he have given him some last night? He'd had off-duty police officers before.

"What time is it?" Blake groaned, struggling into a sitting position.

"Nine-thirty," Jackson told him.

"I usually go to bed at this time." He sat up, yawning.

"Night shift's a bitch."

Blake gave him a sassy look. "I suppose you work nights, too."

"Yep, but I usually keep my clothes on while I'm doing it."

"That's a damn shame," Blake muttered, standing. "Can I use the facilities?"

"Go ahead. Towels are in the closet in the bathroom, behind the door."

"Want to wash my back?" Blake grinned at him. "Or something else?"

"Like I said, I'm no angel, so I'll pass."

"I could take care of any early morning wood you got." Blake leaned across the counter.

"Looks like you got some you need to take care of yourself," he said, glancing down at him.

Blake laughed. "Okay, fine." He walked off to the bathroom. The room was still steamy. It smelled of some woodsy-scented shower gel with a hint of almond. Blake stepped into the shower and turned it on then opened up the shower gel and held it to his nose. Um. As he soaped himself, he couldn't help but imagine Jackson standing naked in this shower with him.

Blake ran his hands over his body with the soapy fragrant gel and stroked his cock. He closed his eyes, the steam making him feel sleepy again. He started to jerk off. As he was coming, he put his forehead against the wet tiles and closed his eyes. He imagined Jackson had walked in and got in behind him. How he wanted to be taken by him, swept away, seized in his powerful arms, filled with passion and longing. "Jackson," he moaned softly. "Yeah, fuck me."

When he finally came out of the bathroom, dressed in yesterday's clothes, Jackson glanced at him. "I was about to come see what had happened to you. You didn't fall into the toilet, did you?"

He laughed. "No. And you would have been welcome to join me."

"You mentioned that already," he murmured.

"I borrowed some shower gel and shampoo. What is that shower gel? It smells really good."

"Some stuff a friend of mine always buys me. It's natural or something. She has a cousin who makes it."

"She?"

"Don't get excited. It's a friend I work with."

"I'm amazed you have friends."

"I guess some people really like torturing themselves." He poured some coffee into a cup and passed it to him. "Cream and sugar are on the counter."

"I take it black." He thanked him and sipped it. "It's good," he said. "A little strong for my taste."

"It's been sitting here while you were jerking off in the shower. No wonder it's strong."

31

"I wasn't jerking off." He stopped there, embarrassed.

"Then you were having some sort of a seizure. Should I call a doctor?"

Blake hid a smile. "Did it turn you on?"

Jackson met his eyes. "Did you intend for it to turn me on?"

"Would have been a fringe benefit." He took another swallow of his coffee.

"Walls are paper-thin here. Can't hide much in this place. And you can refer to me as Jack when you're coming, Jackson takes too much breath."

Blake widened his eyes. Damn. "I didn't say your name."

"Um, my mistake."

"I know other Jacksons."

"Of course," he said. "So, where do you want to go for breakfast?"

"You paying?"

"I've paid for everything else so why stop there?"

"Do you know Dona's?"

"Little place in the Village. It's good. That's fine," Jackson said. "Let's go."

Blake started to pull on his boots.

Jackson reached into the closet and took out a navy three-quartered coat. "What? No ratty khaki coat with a hoodie today?"

Jackson smiled. "No, that was only to impress you. Do you want me to wear it?"

"Ah, no," he muttered. Blake finished putting on his boots.

"You know when I found him," Jackson's voice sliced into the air like a knife cutting through a hard piece of cheese, "there was a bedsheet wrapped around his throat."

Blake turned and looked at him. "What?"

"Tyler," Jackson said. "When I got the call and found him,

he had a sheet wrapped around his throat. I wasn't sure it was even him at first. His face had been so battered, there wasn't much left of it. Most of the bones in his body had been broken. He'd been tortured in every way imaginable, apparently for hours before he died. But he was still wearing the ID bracelet from the Giants game I'd taken him to, three weeks before. It was rather tattered and stained with his blood, but I recognized the logo. I could still see part of the brown football, you know, on the top."

Blake swallowed, staring at him.

"There was a note attached to the pillow beside him. It was addressed to me. It said *Dear Detective Blue. You promised to protect him. Looks like you failed. Don't fuck with me again.* They surmised that the note was written by Tyler. He'd been made to write it during the torture, before all his fingers were broken. The note had his blood on it, too."

Blake felt as if he couldn't get his breath suddenly. "I'm sorry," he said softly. He swallowed the lump in his throat.

"Are you? No one really seemed to care that Tyler was dead. Not the cops, not my partner, not his family. They'd disowned him, thrown him away at fourteen for being gay, born again or some such horseshit. And you certainly don't care either."

Blake sighed. "That's not fair. I am sorry that happened. Truly I am. But you have no proof Manny did it."

"No, no proof, but Manny taunted me with the idea that it was him, challenged me to prove it."

Blake gasped. "What? Manny told you he killed Tyler?"

"On the night I put Manny in the hospital, he told me I was making much ado about nothing, his words, not mine. He'd said, Detective, are you really going to risk your badge over some silly little piece of whore trash? Is it because he had a little crush on you?"

Blake sucked in some air.

"You see, Tyler was dispensable to just about everyone,

including Manny." Jackson paused, looked right at him. "Just like you are dispensable."

"Manny would never hurt me. He has told me how much I mean to him," Blake protested. Anger rose in him.

"That's what he told Tyler, too. That's what he tells all of you. You're all special." Jackson moved closer. "He took you with him because you saw something that could have put him behind bars. He would have killed you, but he couldn't risk it, given that he'd just committed one murder and he knew I was onto him. So, he smothered you with kindness instead. Were you high that night? Is that why the memory is foggy? You were a junkie then, weren't you?"

Blake was shaking. He nodded. "It's the only way I could do some of the stuff I had to do. It made it easier, the cocaine."

"Which Manny supplied in abundance. And where were you the night Tyler died?"

He looked at him. "We were all together that night. Georgie, Tyler, and I, at this party."

"Georgie Hall."

"Yes."

"He can't help us. He's dead. They found him with a needle in his arm a few months later," Jackson told him.

"That's why I kicked the drugs, after they found Georgie."

"Okay. Go on. What happened?"

"I was pretty high. Like I said, Tyler, Georgie, and I were at this party, businessmen types, sick, perverted. I wanted out of there. That was the night Tyler told me about you. That scared me even more to think he was talking to the cops. He said you were different, and he was helping you. He said he loved you, was going to run away with you and marry you. I knew that was just blah blah. I told him he was crazy for talking to the heat."

34

Jackson nodded. "What happened then?"

"Manny arrived. He started accusing one of the men of hurting Tyler. He grabbed Tyler and took him out of there. I remember asking him if I could leave, too, and he said no, I had to stay."

"What time was that?"

"I don't know, one in the morning."

"Did you stay all night then?"

"Yes. I don't remember much after that," Blake said. "When I woke up, I was back at the house we all shared, battered, bruised, and pissed at Manny for taking Tyler and leaving me. It was afternoon. Georgie told me Tyler wasn't there. Two days later, I found out he was dead."

"Georgie say anything else?" Jackson probed.

"No. But he seemed scared, nervous about something. I was too messed up to pursue it."

Jackson walked over and put both hands on Blake's shoulders. "Do you trust me?"

"Should I?"

"Yes, damn it, you should. I know Manny killed Tyler."

"Why? What kind of information did Tyler have that you wanted?"

"Information on a big mobster, one who had taken a shining to Tyler. He spent weekends at his house, was there at meetings with other criminals. Tyler could have helped us take down this guy, and Manny with him."

"You still want this guy?"

"No, he's dead. Listen, Blake, I need you."

Blake pushed Jackson away. He shook his head. "No way. Look what happened to Tyler. You can't ask me to do this. I'm getting out. Manny is going to help me go back to school."

"Bullshit."

"He promised."

"You're delusional." He threw up his hands. "Manny will always have a hold on you. You saw something, something that can tie him to that murder. He thinks one day you just might remember it."

"He's never confessed anything to me, and he's not going to," Blake complained. "He's my ticket out of this life."

"And when is this new life of yours going to begin, because when I last checked you were stripping in front of bunch of old pervs and selling your ass afterwards."

"We're . . . ah . . . discussing it."

"He's just dangling the jewel in front of your eyes. The minute you wise up and try to leave, he'll kill you. He'll probably get one of the mob to do it. They're especially good at that sort of thing."

Blake was shaking. "So, maybe a mobster killed Tyler then." Blake's back was against the wall.

"Nope. That was personal. He did that himself and he enjoyed it." Jackson met his gaze.

"You don't know him like I do."

"I know him better," Jackson said.

"What the fuck you want from me, cop?" He shook his head. "I can't help you. He won't talk about Tyler, and he'll be suspicious if I ask anything."

"I don't want you to ask him. I want you to keep your eyes and ears open. Since Manny has squirmed back up to the surface, he's branched off from running his prostitution racket. He's heavily involved with the drug trade now, taking the place of a former mobster, who ended up dead for betraying the wrong guy. I want you to find out more about that, when the shipments are coming in, and so on. If I can't get him right away for Tyler's murder, I'll put him away for something else. Either way, the bastard will pay."

He'd seen Manny with various members of the Mafia, but he never asked him any questions. This was dangerous. "I'm not doing this," he said, putting on his coat.

Jackson led him out the door. "Doing what? Having breakfast?"

Blake showed him his finger and almost slipped on an icy patch. He swore.

Jackson laughed. "Get in the damn car before you break your neck."

They rode in silence. Blake was getting more and more stressed out. When they got to the Village, Blake said, "You can keep your money—and your proposition." He pushed the money at him. "I'm not snitching on Manny."

Jackson stopped at the intersection and pushed the money back at him. "It's yours."

Blake opened the door. "Have a nice day," he hurled at him.

"I'll meet you in three nights, that all-night coffee shop three blocks from the club, Nightscapes. Maybe you can tell me something then," Jackson told him.

"I won't be there." Blake gave him a defiant look.

"Yes you will," Jackson told him.

Blake slammed the door. *Damn arrogant bastard!* He walked to the corner, finding it hard to stay upright on the icy sidewalk. He was seeking a taxi. He thought he saw one and ran, his hand in the air. The cab was on the other side of the street. Blake tried to cross the intersection only to sink into a huge snowbank. Down he went.

Then Jackson's car pulled to a stop a few feet away from him, the passenger window rolled down.

Blake swore loudly.

"Need a hand there?" Jackson called out, a smirk on his face.

Blake gave him the finger as he tried to struggle out of the snowbank. Each time he got one foot out, the other one went deeper. Damn city.

Cars were blowing their horns behind Jackson. Jackson jumped out of the car and yanked Blake out of the snowbank. "Get in the damn car," he said, "before I back traffic up all the way to Times Square."

Blake limped to the car. He got in the vehicle. "I hate you."

"Why?" Blake turned the corner and sped off in the other direction. "I just pulled you out of the snowbank. That's how you thank someone? This is the Big Apple, not some small town where everyone's related to each other. You might have been there until next week. I was just being a gentleman."

"You were just being a smug asshole." He glared at him.

"So, breakfast or what?" Jackson smiled. "You still don't want to fuck, do you?"

Blake's eyes widened as he stared at him. "You gotta be kidding!"

Jackson burst out laughing.

"Are you always like this?" Blake demanded.

"Just wanted to see how you'd react. Is my charm wearing off yet?"

"Charm? You never had any charm. You have a handsome face, a buff bod, and a big cock, that's it. I never said you were charming," he muttered. "And where in the hell are you taking me anyway?" Blake glanced around.

"You tell me," Jackson said. "I'm at your service. Where do you want to go?"

Blake shook his head. "Can I scream now?"

"Sure, go ahead," Jackson said. "Free country."

They were headed toward the bridge. Where in the world was he taking him?

"I want to go home, I want to eat. And I need to sleep."

"I'll take you now."

"You really think I'm going to take you to where I live?"

"I know where you live anyway."

"How long have you been stalking me?" Blake demanded.

"For a little while, and I wouldn't call it stalking. And may I add, Mr. Wellington, you have one hell of a temper."

"You said you didn't know my name."

Jackson shrugged. "I just remembered it."

"Liar."

# CHAPTER THREE

Blake was not very happy right now. In fact, he was kind of sulking. Jackson didn't give a shit. He was the only link he had to Manny, and come hell or high water, he was going to hang on to it.

"So, you want me to take you to Brooklyn or what?" Jackson asked. The traffic had thinned out across the bridge. He relaxed his hands on the wheel.

"Stop showing off," Blake snapped. "So, you're a good cop, I get it."

"Technically, I'm not a—"

"Right, a suspended cop, who has no intention of letting me off the hook."

"You're pretty bright for a . . . dancer."

"Why not just say cock sucker?"

"That wouldn't be polite, now would it?" Jackson told him.

"I didn't hear you complaining last night," Blake accused.

No, he had no complaint. He wasn't quite sure why he hadn't put a stop to it. He'd told April he was going to find out about Blake's ah . . . talents, but he'd been kidding mostly. Somehow, last night, he'd let Blake get to him. It had been a mistake, because now the memory of Blake's mouth on his cock kept spilling into his mind. Last night, when Blake had come to his room, he'd been so tempted to just invite him into his bed. After he'd left the room, Jackson had been hard as rock. He'd almost gotten up and gone to get him. Since Rob, it had been a series of drunken one-night stands, each less satisfying than the one before. He'd had an active sex life with Rob. Rob loved to be dominated, probably because at work he was always bossing everyone around. They were totally sexually compatible, and their sex life was never boring. It was what he'd missed most when they'd split up. Jackson was pretty sure Blake was also a submissive in bed. Jackson had been so tempted to find out. But he couldn't lose focus. He needed Blake to be his eyes and ears, find him what he needed to put Manny away. He wasn't sure how to convince him to do that, though. Last night, Blake had made it clear he wanted him. It seemed Blake was attracted to him. If that was what it took to get Blake to help him, he'd do it. What would it hurt? Some hot sex, and Manny in prison. It was a win-win situation, wasn't it? Still, not what one could call ethical.

When Jackson pulled into the parking lot of a twenty-four-hour breakfast place off the highway, Blake said, "Breakfast?"

Jackson was hungry, too. "I told you I'd buy you breakfast. I've eaten here before. It's good."

He got out of the car then came around to see that Blake was having some problems.

"Shit, I don't believe this," Blake cried out. "Think I broke my ankle?" He was sitting sideway on the seat.

Jackson went down on his haunches and felt around a little. It was swollen.

"Ow, damn it," Blake said, pushing his hand away.

"Doesn't feel broken. Sprained maybe." Jackson stood. "You should stay off of it."

"Great. How am I supposed to work? I can't dance if I can't put pressure on it." He glanced up at him.

"Lap dances?" Jackson grinned.

"Oh, shut up, and this is all your fault," he accused.

"My fault? I'm not the one who wears boots like that in

the winter." Jackson pointed at Blake's feet. "They have no treads."

"If you hadn't of picked me up, I wouldn't have been there, hailing a cab."

"If it hadn't rained on Sunday, I wouldn't have had to take an umbrella," Jackson mocked.

"Piss off."

Jackson tried to help him, but Blake pushed his arm away. "I'll be all right. I don't need your help."

Jackson watched him hobble to the door. Blake opened it and limped to the first free booth he came to.

Jackson slipped into the seat facing him. "You all right?"

"No. Don't act like you care. Let's eat." Blake looked around.

The waitress came, poured coffee. Blake ordered right away. "Egg white omelet, potatoes, two pieces of whole wheat toast, bacon."

"And you, sir?" she asked, her pencil poised.

"The same for me," Jackson said. "And keep the coffee coming."

She nodded and walked away.

"If you put some ice on it and elevate it," Jackson told him, "you may be able to work tonight if you bandage it. Just don't bop around too much."

Blake swallowed some coffee. "What are you, a doctor now?"

"Sometimes."

The food came. Blake began to wolf it down.

Jackson watched him with a smile. "Need a shovel?"

"Told you I was hungry," he said, spreading some jam on his toast. "So, what's your story?"

"My story?" Jackson echoed, forking some egg into his mouth.

"Yeah, you probably know mine since you seem to know

everything about me," he told him.

"I know nothing much about you. You want to tell me?"

"It's not very interesting. No parents to speak of. Grandmother died when I was young. I was put into a foster home. That didn't work out. So, I was on the streets. Luckily, Manny found me." Blake chewed on some bacon.

"Luckily?" Jackson said under his breath.

"Don't start." He pointed his toast at him.

"That's like saying the rabbit was lucky that the wolf found him so that he wouldn't have to spend a night in the forest by himself." Jackson took another bite of food.

"You have a weird way of seeing things."

Jackson shrugged. The waitress came back to warm up his coffee. He smiled at her. "Thanks."

She smiled back. "Any time."

Blake watched her walk away. "She has the hots for you. You smiled at her, and she almost had an orgasm. You do have a killer smile. Too bad you're so damn annoying."

Jackson lifted an eyebrow. "Sorry about that."

"So, you a New Yorker?"

"Born and raised."

"Let me guess, your father was a cop, too."

"Right on."

"He got you on the force, special privileges, golden boy?"

"You are way off there. He was retired before I got into the academy. He married later in life, after he made lieutenant. He had nothing to do with my career on the force."

"You must have been proud of him."

"I would have been if he'd known how to be a father. He should have never gotten married or had children. He lived and breathed the job, didn't care much for anything or anyone except the NYPD and the bottle."

Blake met his gaze. "I'm sorry," he said, sounding sincere. "So, you weren't close."

"No. We weren't."

"And your mother?"

"She needed me to protect her. She has never been strong. My father was violent sometimes, especially when he drank."

"Sisters? Brothers?"

"One sister, rather a lost cause. So," Jackson said, wanting to change the subject, "does that mean we've bonded now and you'll help me with Manny?"

"That was a nice moment. Did you have to ruin it?" Blake put down his folk. "You really are an asshole sometimes. Modeled from the old man?"

That pissed Jackson off. "Listen, I don't give a fuck what you think of me, Blake. I really need to put Manny away and I can't do it alone." He leaned across the table.

Blake leaned back. "You are obsessed with Manny. And I said no. Whatcha going to do about it?"

Jackson sighed. Damn it. Suddenly, he said, "Beg, if I have to." He sat back. Damn it. He'd told this guy more than he'd told the stupid police shrink.

Blake opened his mouth to speak then closed it.

They sat in silence for a little while. Blake had no idea what Tyler's death had cost Jackson, or how not avenging Tyler's death would eventually destroy him. Would it make any difference to him if he tried to explain it?

When Blake reached over and put his hand over Jackson's, Jackson raised an eyebrow.

"You don't have to say it. It's in your eyes," Blake said softly. "But what if you're wrong?"

"I'm not wrong."

Blake left his hand there for a few more seconds then removed it. "Why did Tyler mean so much to you? I'm sure you've had to deal with other murders on the force. You identified with him?"

"He was a little boy lost. Maybe I was the same at his age, feeling like I was all alone in the world."

"Do you still feel that way?" Blake asked. "Lost?"

"Sometimes. You?"

Blake examined his hands. "If not for Manny." He picked up his head again. "Listen, if I see or hear anything that I think can help you, I'll tell you. But it doesn't mean I report everything."

That wasn't going to work. "You may not think something is important when it is," Jackson insisted. "No, Blake, you need to tell me everything. Who he talks to, where he goes. You are either in this or you're not. You're the closest thing to Manny I got. What will it take for you to help me?"

Blake didn't comment.

That worried him. "Come back to my place. I'll fix your ankle then drive you to work tonight." Jackson waited for Blake to agree. He wasn't sure what would happen. He'd seduce him if he had to. But Jackson wasn't even sure that would work. Blake was definitely attached to Manny emotionally. And in some bizarre way, Manny had done good by Blake. But he'd killed Tyler, and that was all Jackson cared about.

Jackson helped Blake into the car. They rode in silence until they got back to Jackson's place.

"I can't believe you talked me into coming back here," Blake confessed as Jackson helped him settle onto the sofa.

"Listen, you blamed me for hurting yourself, so I guess it's my job to fix you up." Jackson walked to the refrigerator. "Can you get your boot off?"

"Yeah, I'm doing that now. Ouch, that hurt," he murmured.

Jackson lifted Blake's leg up onto the sofa and put a cushion under his foot. He sat on the coffee table and ran his fingers over the darkening discoloration. "Yeah, it's starting to bruise. Let's see if we can get the swelling down," he said. He'd wrapped the ice pack in a towel. He turned Blake's leg a little to the left and gently put the ice pack on his ankle. "Try not to move," he said, reaching over and propping more cushions under Blake's back. "I'll get you some aspirin for the pain."

"No," he said. "I don't take any drugs."

"Not even a pain killer?"

"Nothing."

"I'll see if I can find a bandage in the medicine cabinet." Jackson stood and went to rummage in the bathroom. When he came out with the elastic bandage, his phone was vibrating. There was a shitload of messages on there. "You okay?" he asked, picking up the phone.

"Yeah, fine."

"Found the bandage. We'll do the ice for a bit then bandage it later." Jackson scrolled down his messages. Latest ones were from April. He'd better phone her before she turned up at his door. "I'm just going to make a call," he said.

"Okay."

April picked up right away. "Jack? Are you all right?"

"Fine."

"I've been trying to reach you all morning. Did you speak to the lieutenant yet?"

"No. What does she want?"

"They want you back at work."

"What about Internal Affairs?" he asked.

"Bigger fish. The charges were dropped."

"That's strange," he said.

"Well, you can figure that out later. We may have a serial killer on our hands. Remember that young boy they found three months ago in the river?"

"Yeah. He was a hustler."

"Well, we got another one, same MO. Seems our killer is

targeting young, male prostitutes. There was a note sent to the precinct. It said he was enjoying it and intends on doing it again soon. We need you on that task force, Jack. You know this world."

"What about the charge of excessive force? I don't get it. Why would he drop the charges? The guy was an ass."

"I don't know. All I know is, she wants you to come in. She was in a shit mood yesterday. Told me to find you and get you in here."

"I'll be there later today."

"Jackson, you need to—"

He hung up. A few minutes later, he came around to the sofa to see that Blake had fallen asleep. Damn. He sat on the coffee table and removed the ice pack. The ankle looked less puffy. He went to the freezer and took out another ice pack.

He wrapped the pack and came over to set it on his ankle again. As he did, Blake's fingers ruffled his hair. He looked at him. "Thought you were asleep."

His fingers trailed down to Jackson's cheekbone then to his jaw. Jackson didn't know what to do. He just kind of froze. Blake moved one finger up to Jackson's bottom lip and traced it, then he withdrew his hand. Their gazes met and locked. Blake visibly swallowed. Jackson lowered his head, moving closer to his face. He'd almost kissed him, then he remembered Blake said he didn't kiss.

Abruptly he stood, took a step back. "The ice is helping," he managed.

"Got an ice pack for this?" he asked softly, framing the tent in his pants with his hand.

Jackson licked his bottom lip. His breathing grew shallow. "Don't do this to me," he pleaded.

"Do what?" he asked softly. "Want you?"

"Yeah, that," he said.

"Well, I think you have the advantage. I'm just lying here.

I can't move, which means I can't do anything about it. I'm completely in your power."

The lust in Blake's eyes was enough to make Jackson rip off the guy's clothes then and there.

Blake undid the zipper on his pants and slipped his hand into his pants, stroking his cock. He never took his gaze away from Jackson. "You make me so hot. I don't know why. Jesus. I don't even like you very much."

"I don't like you either," Jackson breathed, watching him stroke his own cock. "Very much," he added.

"It's a match made in Heaven then," Blake murmured as his head went back and he grunted.

"Goddamn it," Jackson whispered. He reached out and pulled Blake up off the sofa. There wasn't any resistance as he threw him over his shoulder. When he lay him down on the bed, they were both breathing hard.

Jackson tore off his shirt while Blake silently watched him. He undid his pants and pushed them down over his hips, leaving them in a pile on the floor. The underwear came next with the socks.

Jackson put a knee on the bed and grabbed the material of Blake's t-shirt at the collar and ripped it down the middle. Then he proceeded to take off the leather pants. Blake wasn't wearing underwear. Jackson swept his gaze over him. Blake's cock was hard, standing upright in invitation, his balls heavy. Jackson straddled Blake's thighs, ran both hands up Blake's chest, pausing to tweak each nipple.

Blake made a sound of pleasure in his throat. Jackson rubbed his thumbs over them, then rolled them between thumb and forefingers, pulling on them while he moved his hips, making sure his own erection was brushing against Blake's.

Blake let his head go back into the pillow. He moaned softly.

"You like that," Jackson murmured. "You have sensitive nipples." He leaned down and laved his tongue over one of them.

Black reached up and threaded his fingers in Jackson's hair, keeping his mouth there. Jackson brought his head back up. He grabbed Blake's wrists and pressed them against the mattress, looking down into his eyes. Blake's chest heaved.

"You're not in charge. I am. I'll do whatever I want to you. And you'll do whatever I say."

Blake licked his lips. He nodded, a faint smile forming on his lips. Blake released his wrists. "My ex used to love it when I tied his wrists. I used to clamp his nipples and slip on a cock ring. I still have the sex toys."

Blake nodded. "Oh yeah," he said softly. "I'm yours."

Jackson reached over into the night table. He brought out lube, condoms, nipple clamps, a cock ring, and a double-headed vibrating dildo. In the top drawer were his hand-cuffs. He dangled them in front of Blake.

"Have I been a bad boy, Officer?" His eyes were shining.

Jackson turned on the dildo. He reached down and let it vibrate next to Blake's cock. He leaned over and attached Blake's wrists to the bedpost, letting his hands trail down over his chest after he did.

He reared back and pushed Blake's legs farther apart and lightly played with his erection.

"Um," Blake murmured.

He got a bit rougher, cuffing Blake's glistening rod a little. Then he slipped on the cock ring. Blake admired his handi-work as he rubbed lube on his hands. Jackson stroked his own cock with the lube while Blake watched, his hips lifting a few times. Then Jackson rubbed the lube over his own chest then over Blake's nipples before he gripped them in silver clamps.

"That feel good?" Jackson asked as he studied the expression on Blake's face, a mix of pain and pleasure.

"Um, yeah," Blake replied, running his hands over Jackson's thighs.

Jackson held up the dildo. He took his time rubbing lube over it then lifted Blake's legs onto his shoulders. Jackson spiraled the vibrator around Blake's anus then pushed.

Blake let out a cry. "Oh yeah, damn it, Jackson, um."

Jackson chuckled softly. He pushed it deeper, pulling it in and out a few times then left it vibrating inside him. "You are so beautiful," Jackson told him. "You want to come badly."

Blake lifted his hips. "You are one bad boy."

"No, you are," he said. "And you're going to suck my cock now." Jackson moved up over his chest, tugging on the nipple clamps a few times.

Blake groaned and opened his mouth when Jackson positioned the pillow so he could lower his cock deeper into Blake's throat. Jackson's cock was being completely consumed by Blake's expert mouth. Damn. He was good at that.

"Okay, okay," Jackson told him. "I don't want to come in your mouth. I want to come inside you."

Blake let him back out, nodding. "Oh yeah, fuck me, Jackson. Fuck me."

Jackson played with the nipple clamps for a moment then removed the cock ring. He stroked Blake a few times as he withdrew the vibrator, turning it off and throwing it aside. He undid the handcuffs and handed Blake a condom. "Put it on me," he breathed.

Blake sat up and ripped open the package. His hands were shaking as he pulled it out. Jackson sat on his knees in front of him, his eyes closing as the condom slipped up over his cock.

Jackson roughly turned Blake around, bringing him to his

knees. He propelled his head down and positioned himself. "Oh, you are all nice and open for me." He pressed his lips against Blake's ear. "Baby . . ." He slapped his ass and pushed his cock into him. One hand held his head down, the other played with the nipple clamps as he fucked him hard-core. Deep and fast, then slow then fast again, the sounds of their fucking bounced off the walls.

Blake was shouting something. Jackson took Blake's cock in his hand and felt the come run through his fingers, his body alive with the sensation. The feeling of elation reverberated through him, going straight to his core.

He fell back on the bed, his breathing hard, spent, his body feeling like a limp noodle. But he felt alive, happy. Reconnected.

Blake lay on his stomach a little way away. Jackson wanted to move closer, touch him. Damn it, he wanted to kiss him. But he wouldn't.

Blake turned his head, looked at him. "Man, you can fuck."

Jackson smiled. "I assume that's a compliment."

"Coming from me, yeah. You know how many men I've had to compare—"

"No." Jackson sat up, shaking his head. "I don't want to know either."

"Oh, okay. I just meant that—"

"Yeah, that you have a lot to compare me to. Glad I measured up." It came out sounding weird. "And this shouldn't be weird. Just two guys fucking. Right?"

Blake said, "Yeah, sure. I didn't think it was more than that. Did you?"

"No." Jackson got off the bed. He picked up the toys and put them on his nightstand.

"Have you had a lot of lovers?" Blake asked him.

"Enough. Too many, probably," Jackson said. "Nothing

compared to you."

Blake nodded. "Ever love any of them?"

"I don't know, maybe. I thought I loved Rob."

"He lived here with you?"

"No. I lived with him in a house. I left him."

"Why?"

Blake shrugged. "I don't really want to talk about Rob."

"Because you still love him?" Blake was staring at him.

"No. Now, can we change the subject?"

"Okay."

"How's the ankle?" Jackson came over to examine it. He let his fingers run over it. When he glanced up, Blake was looking at him. "What?" he said.

"Nothing." Blake smiled at him. "You're too handsome to be a cop."

Jackson smiled. "Listen, I have to drive you home. I'm needed at the station. I guess I can't put it off too much longer. The lieutenant is going nuts."

"No problem," Blake told him. "So, guess they are reinstating their bad-boy officer?"

"Something like that," Jackson said.

An hour later, Jackson pulled up outside Blake's apartment building. "Thanks for the ride. I think I'll call the club and stay home tonight."

"Might be a good idea."

"So, what happened with your suspension anyway?"

"I don't know. My friend told me the charges were dropped. Maybe he realized he deserved the punch in the mouth I gave him."

Blake smiled faintly. "Who was he?"

"The father of a teenager we found dead. He'd been murdered. When I tracked him down to tell him about his son, he said it was justice because his son was queer. I didn't like that much so I slugged him."

Blake touched his arm. "Are you trying to get me to fall in love with you?"

Jackson's eyes widened. That took him aback. "Ah, no."

Blake lowered his head for a moment. "Then stop doing things like that."

"Listen," Jackson said. "We may have a serial killer out there targeting male prostitutes. Watch yourself, okay?"

"I don't stand on the street corners anymore, Jackson. And I'm always careful. With this case, does that mean your obsession with Manny is over then?"

"Never," Jackson said, shaking his head. "Are you going to help me?"

"Is that why you had sex with me, so that I'd help you?"

"Maybe." Jackson told him. "Did it work?"

"Maybe," Blake echoed.

Jackson laughed, watching as he opened the door. "Do you need help?"

"No, I'm fine. Thanks. I'll do what I can. We still on three nights from now at the café?"

"I'll call you."

Blake raised a hand and turned away. Jackson watched him limp up the path to his building and disappear inside. Maybe this was the last he'd see him. There were really no circumstances under which he could force Blake to help him bring down Manny. And aside from shooting Manny in the head, he'd never pay for Tyler's murder until Jackson had something he could use to put him away.

On the way to the police station, his mind was on something else. Why had that creep dropped charges against him? This was twice now, first because Manny had run off, frightened by something, and now, another cretin decided it wasn't worth the effort. Either he was one lucky son of a bitch or something was going on.

The lieutenant waved him into her office the minute he

arrived. A tall, athletic woman with curly dark hair, attractive enough, twice divorced. She had the phone cradled between her shoulder and ear as she tapped away on the keyboard. Jackson closed the door behind him, glancing around at the pictures of her twin teenage girls that peppered the wall.

Lieutenant Janet Delany was tough as nails. She'd had to be to make it as far as she had in such a misogynist hierarchy. But as tough as she was, she was fair, and clever as a fox. They'd had their run-ins, but he wouldn't want to see someone else in her place.

The lieutenant put down the phone. "Well, long time no see, Sergeant Blue."

"I suppose I'm in deep shit," he said with a faint smile.

"Oh, you are way beyond being in deep shit, Jackson. The only reason I don't fire your perfect ass is because you are one of the finest cops in this division."

"Oh, a compliment," he said, clearing his throat. "And thanks for noticing my ass."

She pointed at him. "Don't get cocky. I might just change my mind. Between you and me, you know, if I'd been there with that creep and he'd said what he'd said about his son after identifying the body, I would have felt like slugging him, too."

Jackson remained silent.

"However," she said. "The difference between me and you is, I would have restrained myself."

Jackson lifted his head. "I did apologize."

She nodded. "Yeah. You dislocated his jaw and gave him two black eyes, Jackson."

"Why did he drop the charges then?"

She sat back in her chair. "I asked him to."

Jackson raised an eyebrow. "I don't understand. Isn't that not quite ethical?"

"Fuck the ethics," she said. "I told him that the same killer who'd murdered his son was probably at it again and that you were the only cop who could stop him. I blamed it on overwork and too much drinking, and that you have a shitty disposition."

"Oh. Ah, thank you, I think."

"As a former drinker himself and a sponsor, he showed compassion. You are to stay away from him, understood?" She pointed at him, pushing his gun and badge toward him across the desk.

"It's not like we'll have lunch or anything."

"Right." She turned the computer screen around on her desk. "Take your gun and badge back and then come and have a look," she said.

Jackson picked them up and moved closer to the screen. He studied the pictures of the crime scene. "Strangled," he said. Bruising marred the boy's neck. He was still bloated from being pulled from the water. "Same vicinity?"

"Within a mile," she said. "Weighted down by an anchor beside the dock, like the first victim. Almost missed it. River is still frozen in places."

"Forensic results back yet?" he asked.

"No, we're waiting on them. This one is a John Doe. We don't know who he is yet. We're working on it."

"No one see anything?"

"There was a security guard at night. He was asked a few questions, needs to be asked again. He isn't the sharpest tack. The camera footage seems defective. We're checking it now. We haven't found anyone else. He was dumped in the wee hours of the morning." She tapped something into the keyboard. "Here is the letter we received hours after the murder."

Jackson read it aloud.

"*Dear Detective. Here is number two. I really enjoyed doing this one. There will be more coming. Happy hunting. Your secret admirer."*

"One sick fuck," he said.

"You got that right."

"Why, dear detective, and not detectives?"

"We don't know. Maybe he is thinking of one particular detective."

"It's a clue he's giving us. Do you think it's me he's writing to?"

"Why? You weren't the only cop on the first victim's task force."

No, but he was the only cop left who worked on Tyler's case. He wasn't ready to say that yet, but what if there was a connection?

"There's no time to waste. Three months since the last one. We don't know if he'll stick to that timeline or not." She turned the screen back to face her. "Jackson, I want you and April Grant heading up the task force. You can have anyone else on it you want. Just find this creep. I'm transferring the files to you now."

It was two in the morning before he left the precinct. He and April had been working out their strategy and choosing the members of the task force, fueled by bad coffee and cold pizza. Tomorrow would be their first meeting.

The next two days just sped by. They revisited the crime scene, questioned anyone in the area who may have seen anything, and revisited the camera footage at the docks. All the while, Jackson waited on the forensic report.

He almost forgot about his meeting with Blake at the café. At the last minute, he drove all the way down there, only to sit around for an hour, alone. Blake never showed up. "Damn it," he said under his breath. The club was closed. Blake could be anywhere, and with anyone.

Jackson got into his car and drove to Brooklyn. He took a chance that Blake was there, at home. Sure enough, there was a light on in his apartment. Jackson got out of the car and jogged up the path. It was a security building, but luckily some guy was coming through the lobby. He held the door open. "Sorry, I forget my keys," he said.

The guy didn't look twice. He just kept on going.

A few minutes later, Jackson was standing in front of Blake's apartment door. Someone was talking, and music played low. He rang the bell.

The door opened. Blake stood there. "Hey."

"You stood me up," Jackson told him.

"Were we supposed to meet? You said you'd call." Blake looked over his shoulder.

"Am I interrupting something? Got a hot date?"

A young man came walking down the hall, tall and thin, with short blond hair. "Hello," he said, smiling at Jackson.

Jackson nodded.

The man reached past Blake and pulled Jackson inside. "You're so rude, Blake. Invite the man in."

Jackson found himself standing in the hallway. Blake closed the door behind him.

"My, my, you are one handsome man, and built. You work out?" He was rubbing Jackson's arm.

Blake winced. "Colin, ah, stop that."

Colin removed his hand like someone had slapped it. "Oh, sorry."

Jackson addressed himself to Blake. "I waited at the café for you. You never showed."

"You look tired," Blake said. "Can I get you something?"

"Don't change the subject."

Colin wandered off down the hallway.

"Who is he anyway?" Jackson asked.

"Ah, my boyfriend, kind of," Blake mumbled.

"Boyfriend?" Jackson met his gaze. "It would have been nice of you to tell me you had a boyfriend before I fucked the hell out of your ass."

"You didn't ask," he said. "And anyway, it's okay with Colin, you paid. He doesn't."

Jackson sucked in some air. "Yeah, overpaid, now *that* I remember."

Blake raised his voice. "Fuck you, you know."

"Did that already. We need to talk."

"I'm a little busy."

"Well, clear your schedule," Jackson told him, taking his arm and steering him into the bedroom. He closed the door.

"Hey." Blake pulled his arm away. "Don't manhandle me. I'm not a suspect. Listen, I considered what you said, and I decided I don't want to get involved with any of it." He took a few steps back. "Manny is your obsession, not mine. I'm trying to keep my distance."

"Why, if he's such a good pal of yours?" Jackson sneered.

"I want to live a different life, go to school, stop taking my clothes off for perverts. I don't take any money from Manny. I pay this place by myself."

"Not from dancing you don't."

"Okay, so I have a few high-paying clients. They're discreet, safe. They pay me enough to make the rent for two, three months sometimes."

Jackson folded his arms across his chest. "Talk to me."

Blake shook his head. "And then it's over?" He met his gaze. "I mean, you won't bother me anymore?"

"You'll never have to see me again if that's what you want."

There was a long silence. Blake took a few steps toward him, stopped. "Maybe I want to see you."

"Listen, Blake, fuck you with this stuff. Don't play games with me. Your boyfriend is waiting in the hallway."

Blake reached out to touch his cheek.

Jackson batted his hand away. "Don't touch me."

Blake sighed. "Manny has someone he protects from the

outside world."

Jackson raised an eyebrow. "Go on. Who is it, and why is he protecting him? Do you know this person?"

"A few years back. Haven't seen him in a while."

"Was he one of Manny's hustlers?"

"No. He never worked the streets."

"What was his name?"

"Manny called him" — he paused — "ah, Jack, I think."

"Jack? He called him Jack?" Was that some kind of a sick joke?

Blake nodded. "Jack was a little strange. He was really quiet, followed me all over the place."

"And what did Jack call Manny?"

"He called him Manny. I saw Jack a few years ago, when Tyler was killed. Manny asked me to hang out with him, keep him company. He was about fifteen years old then. He gave me the creeps."

"Why? What was creepy about him?"

"The way he kept staring at me, something about his eyes. Anyway, I saw him a few times after that before he kind of disappeared."

"What do you mean, he kind of disappeared?"

"Well, it was like he was around, but he wasn't. I didn't see him."

"Did he become a ghost?" Jackson demanded.

"Funny guy. No. He didn't die or anything. Manny referred to him every once in a while. He said he'd bought him this and that, had lunch with him, but he was just out of sight."

"Could you describe him?"

"Yes, when he was fifteen, not now. That was a few years ago. Jackson, listen, I swore to Manny I wouldn't talk about Jack to anyone. You can't tell him I told you this."

"Why would I tell Manny anything that might put you in

harm's way? It's not like Manny and I hang together."

"I'm not sure this will help you."

"I told you, things you may think are insignificant can be important in a murder investigation. You need to tell me more about this Jack guy. Why in hell didn't you mention him before?"

He shrugged. "Listen, I can send Colin home. We could be alone to—talk." Blake met Jackson's gaze.

Jackson understood his message well enough. He moaned inwardly. Yes, oh yes. He wanted to fuck him again badly, but he had to put the brakes on. "Just to talk," he said, not sure he even believed his own words.

Blake nodded. "I'll tell Colin. He just moved in downstairs."

"How convenient," Jackson replied, undoing his jacket. "And already your boyfriend?"

"I'll make coffee. Want some?" Blake asked, opening the door.

"I could use something stronger," he said.

Blake nodded. "Okay."

Colin was gone when they walked out of the room.

Blake locked the door. "Oh well. I'll pour you a drink," he said. "What's your poison?"

"Scotch if you have it, straight up." Jackson followed him down the hallway and into the living room. It was nice, cozy, a tiny kitchen and bathroom on the right. Even a small apartment like this could cost a pretty penny in New York.

Jackson walked to the window. "Nice view," he said.

Blake came up behind him. "Yes," he replied, running his gaze over the length of Jackson. "It sure is."

Jackson took the drink from his hand. "I was talking about the view from the window."

"So was I," Blake said with a grin, raising his own glass.

Jackson took a sip. If he got out of here tonight without

removing his clothes, it was going to be a damn miracle.

# CHAPTER FOUR

Blake had to have him tonight. In fact, he'd thought of nothing else since they'd been together almost three days ago. Colin wasn't his boyfriend anyway. He'd just moved in a few weeks ago and he seemed lonely, always coming by to borrow this or that. Seemed innocent enough. Anyway, it was fun to see the reaction from Jackson when he'd said that. Blake was sure he was jealous, and deep down, it pleased him.

He moved closer. "Haven't I earned something?" He watched Jackson take another deep swallow from the glass.

"That depends," he said.

The golden liquor was glistening on his lips. It was driving Blake to distraction. He wanted to kiss that mouth. It was insane. Was he about to break his golden rule? His gaze settled on that mouth. "Depends on what?" he asked softly. He could hardly breathe.

"On what else you tell me about this Jack."

"And if I tell you everything, what do I get then?" He reached up and stroked back his hair.

"Probably a hell of a lot more than you can handle," Jackson told him.

"I can handle anything you got, baby," Blake replied, taking Jackson's empty glass and putting it on the coffee table. He drained his own and he let it fall to the carpet as he wound his arms around Jackson's neck. Jackson's hard cock pressed against his stomach. He closed the space between them. "You're hard."

Jackson was breathing heavy. His hands moved down Blake's back to his ass. He squeezed his ass cheeks as he lowered his face to Blake's neck. "You're going to be the death of me," he whispered in his ear. "I've never wanted anyone this much before. "Are you a sorcerer?"

Blake smiled. "No. But I'm yours, so show me whatcha got."

"Damn it," Jackson grunted. He pulled Blake's t-shirt over his head and then reached for the jeans. Hastily he unzipped them and took them down. Blake stepped out of them. "Again, no underwear?" Jackson smiled. "I do like your style." Jackson wrapped his fist around Blake's erection and brought him closer.

Blake gasped.

Jackson's hand released Blake's cock and clamped down onto his shoulder, pressing him to his knees. Jackson undid his pants, took them off along with his underwear, and stepped out of them.

Blake watched him for a moment as he stroked his own cock. He licked his lips, wanting to taste him so badly.

Jackson placed a hand on Blake's forehead and pushed his head back. Straddling him, he let his cock slide along Blake's lips. Blake moaned softly, catching the pre-come with the tip of his tongue.

"You're so hot," Blake whispered, opening his mouth.

Jackson lowered his cock into his mouth, teasingly, moving farther in then lifting up again as if he were fucking his mouth. Blake sucked and licked each time. Jackson moved from side to side then went deeper into Blake's throat. It was so erotic. Jackson was so sexy.

Blake raised his hand to play with Jackson's balls, rolling them between his fingers when he swallowed more of him.

Jackson's legs were unsteady, trembling. His hands moved in Blake's hair, and he cried out something. It sounded like he might be praying. Blake sucked harder. A few minutes later, Jackson was coming, his cock pulsing in Blake's mouth.

Blake swallowed, opened up as wide as he could. Jackson's cock pulled back. He cried out.

"Yes, fuck, yes." Jackson's hips bucked against Blake's mouth.

Jackson stumbled back a few feet, his hand on his cock as he slammed against the wall. "Jesus God," he said, his chest heaving.

Blake got to his feet, wiping his mouth on the back of his hand. He watched him. Damn, did he have to be the most beautiful man he'd ever seen? Blake walked over and began to undo Jackson's shirt. It slipped off his shoulders and fell to the floor. He ran his fingertips over his chest, his biceps, the wavy knots of abdominals. He put his lips there, licking at his nipples, reaching down to fondle his dwindling cock.

Jackson grabbed Blake's hair in his fist, again tipping his head back. He looked into his eyes. "Kiss me," he said gruffly.

Blake opened his mouth. He was about to say something, but he didn't have a chance. Jackson's mouth came crashing down on his, hard, forcing it to open to his. Their tongues met, battled, slid around each other's.

Blake struggled to get closer, melding his body to his, moving one hand up into Jackson's hair, clawing at his back with the other. He wanted more, more of his mouth, of his hot kisses. Jackson's mouth was devouring him, and if he could have crawled inside the man, he would have.

Jackson released him.

Blake stood stunned for a moment. He'd been deeply affected, damaged by those damn kisses. *Bastard.*

"I'm going to fuck you now," Jackson told him. He grabbed him and turned him around, tipping him over the sofa. Jackson nudged Blake's knees far apart. There was the sound of a condom packet ripping. "Where's the lube?" he asked.

"In the bedroom, the night table." Blake closed his eyes, his cock stiffening in anticipation.

"Don't move."

He wasn't going anywhere.

A few minutes later, Jackson came back. "I found all kinds of good stuff in there," he said. Jackson slapped Blake's ass a few times then skewered a lubed finger up into his anus.

Blake grunted, making sounds of pleasure as Jackson fucked him with one finger, then two, then four. In and out, slowly, while the other hand lightly smacked his ass.

Jackson pulled his fingers out and lifted Blake's head. He turned him around and lowered his mouth to Blake's chest and, grabbing his nipple between his teeth, he pulled and sucked them.

Blake was close to screaming, his cock leaking come.

Jackson cuffed his cock a few times. "Be a good boy," he said. "Can't come yet." He lifted a pair of nipple clamps off the sofa. They were his favorites, drooping diamonds, and they had a particularly hard bite on them.

Jackson pinched one nipple and clamped it.

Blake swooned. "Um, yeah, so good."

He teased the other one then did the same. He stood admiring his handiwork for a few minutes then played with the clamps, tugging with his teeth, sending shockwaves through Blake.

A few more cuffs on the cock, then Jackson pointed to the carpet. "On your knees, ass up, legs spread."

Blake eagerly dropped to his knees. "Tell me what you are going to do," he pleaded, licking his lips. "Where are you going to put that big, hard cock?"

"I'm going to fuck your tight little ass so hard and so deep, you're going to taste my cock in your mouth," he said. "I'm going to make you scream, beautiful slut."

Jackson's hand grabbed the back of his neck and pushed his head down. He didn't hesitate. He plunged into his ass, hard and fast with his cock. It was as pretty damn close to Heaven as he was ever going to get.

Later, Blake lay on his stomach on the carpet, trying to get a breath. He'd come so hard, it felt as if he'd been the one drained this time. Jackson was gathering his clothes together. "You're not leaving?" Blake looked up at him.

"No, not yet," he said. "You promised to tell me more about Jack."

Blake sat up. "Is that all it is? This? Between us right now? Just to get information? So, who's the real hustler here, you or me?"

Jackson zipped up his jeans. He sunk into the chair across from him. "We're all hustlers."

Blake swallowed. Why did he care? It was just sex. He didn't want to care like this about anyone. "You will never own me."

Jackson sighed. "I don't want to own you."

"Just saying. You'll never make me care so much that I—"

Jackson narrowed his eyes. "What are you saying, Blake?"

"Nothing, fuck all. Never mind. Anyway, what else do you want to know about him?"

"What did he look like? Did he look like Manny?"

Blake sighed. "A little."

"It's his son, right?" Jackson met his gaze.

"I suppose, yeah. Not sure."

"So, does he look like Manny or not? Dark hair, short, Italian?"

Blake got to his feet. "No, not really. He had reddish hair, my height, thin."

"Was he gay, straight?"

"I don't know. Like I said, just creepy."

Jackson put his shirt on.

"He didn't seem to have a personality. He always wanted to know what I wanted to do, and he would go along with it." Blake pulled on his pants.

"You said he was around at the time of Tyler's murder?"

"Yes. How many times you going to ask me that, Jackson?"

"How long after that before he disappeared? Was it the same time?"

"Could have been. I think so. I don't remember seeing him anymore after that."

"Did you ever ask Manny what happened to him?" Jackson asked.

"You learn not to question Manny too much. He doesn't like it." Blake walked to the kitchen. "You want coffee?"

"No. I'm leaving," Jackson replied. "I need to get some sleep."

Blake turned to look at him. "You want me to find out where Jack is, don't you?"

Jackson came closer.

"I'll find a way to ask him. How is your case going?"

"Slowly, like they usually do." Jackson slipped on his jacket.

"I'm sorry I didn't meet you," Blake blurted out as Jackson headed to the door. The clock on the wall said it was almost four in the morning.

Jackson paused. "No, you're not," he said. "You do exactly as you want to do."

Blake smiled. "Okay." He walked over and slid the lock off the door. "So, when am I going to see you again?"

"I'll call you," Jackson said.

"Do you even have my number?" he asked.

"Yeah," Jackson replied. "I took it off your phone the first night we met."

"Why am I not surprised?"

Jackson handed him his card. "If you need to get in touch with me."

Blake took it. "Sergeant Blue, Detectives' Division," he read. "Impressive."

Jackson put his hand on the door handle. "Be careful, Blake. It's dangerous out there." He turned the handle and opened the door.

Blake locked the door after Jackson left. He went to the window and watched him walk out to his car. Blake could still feel his hot kisses on his mouth. He closed his eyes. He could fall for him big time if he didn't keep himself in check. Jackson confused him, made him feel off balance. He didn't like that feeling. It made him feel as if he'd lost control. When he was in Jackson's arms, the world went away.

Blake waited until his car drove away then sat on the sofa. He closed his eyes. He wasn't sure what it was between them and he didn't want to question it. His eyes were closing. He grabbed a cushion and put his head on it, drifting off to sleep.

The sound of his doorbell ringing woke him. He checked the time. Almost one in the afternoon. Maybe it was Jackson. Why in the hell would it be? Damn, he had Jackson on the brain.

It was Manny. It took him aback for a few minutes. It was rare Manny showed up at his place.

"Hey, kid," he said. "You don't seem happy to see me."

"Of course I am," Blake replied. "Come in."

"Looks like I woke you." He glanced around the apartment. "Have company last night?"

"Just Colin."

Manny pursed his lips. "You're lying to me."

Blake swallowed. "What? No."

"You were with Jackson Blue last night." He took a seat. "What I want to know is why?"

"Is that his name?" Blake shrugged. "That's not what he told me. Used an alias. Anyway, johns are rarely honest. Said his name was Mark. Never did get a last name."

"How did you meet him?"

Blake was fighting the urge to run. He was terrified. *Keep cool. Don't show fear.* "Ah, he picked me up on the street, after the club. He paid well. Heard about my talent for blow jobs."

Manny nodded. "He's a cop."

"A . . . what?" Blake asked, hoping he looked confused. "No. I mean, how can he be?"

"Did he ask you anything about me?" Manny stood, eyeing him.

Blake was standing behind the sofa. He was gripping the top of it. "No. He paid his money, we did the nasty, and that was it."

"He was here a long time for that."

"He paid double. Likes to take his time." Blake walked over to the kitchen counter. He'd put the money Jackson had given him in a jar in the cupboard. He took out four hundred. "See." He showed Manny the bills.

"I don't want you seeing him again," Manny said, ignoring the money.

"I thought you said that I was free to do what I wanted now?" Blake stiffened. Maybe Jackson had been right after all.

"Of course." He smiled. "You need to understand something. That cop has a beef with me. He's trying to get information from you. Stay away."

"I didn't tell him anything. I don't know anything." Blake shook his head. "And even if I did, I'd never blab to a cop.

You know that, Manny. I love you."

Manny came closer. He reached out and drew Blake into his embrace. He hugged him a little too hard. "You better mean that, Blake. Anything else, I mean, if I ever thought you would betray me, well, I don't know what I'd be capable of."

Blake nodded, shaking like a leaf.

Manny released him, smiling. "Well, now that that's settled . . ."

"Ah," Blake said, "how did you know that cop was here last night? Have you been watching me?"

"Blake. I always make sure you're protected." He walked to the door. "I'd just be devastated if something was to happen to you."

The door opened and closed. Blake sat on the sofa and put his face in his hands. He picked up the phone and dialed Jackson's number.

He got his phone mail. "Detective Blue. Leave a message, your number, and I'll get back to you."

"Ah, Jackson, Blake. Listen, Manny was here. He knew we were together. I'm a little freaked right now. Can you call me back?" He hung up. When the doorbell rang again, he almost jumped out of his skin. "Jackson," he said, running to the door. He opened it to see Colin standing there. "Oh, hi," he said, a little disappointed.

"Hoping for someone else?"

"No, no, come in."

"Hey. You okay?" Colin rubbed Blake's arm.

"Yeah, fine."

"The hunk gone?" Colin walked in and closed the door behind him.

"Yeah," Blake replied, smiling at Colin's description.

"It serious between you and the cop?"

Blake blinked. "How did you know he was a cop? Did I

say that?"

Colin shrugged. "I can tell. And you mentioned it. Ah, he was wearing a badge."

He'd have to be more careful. "Ah, no, not serious. Just a client," Blake said hastily.

"So, who spooked you?"

"No one. I'm fine. Just woke up, that's all."

"Listen, I'll pour us a couple of drinks, and then we'll talk, okay?" Colin said. "Sit down, relax. You can pour your heart out about the hunk."

"Like I said, just a client." Blake looked at his phone sitting on the coffee table. *Come on, Jackson, call me back.* "I have to get ready for work, so I'll pass on the drink."

"You sure? One drink, that's all. It will relax you."

"No," Blake said, "thanks."

"So, what's the real story with you and the cop?" Colin asked. "Come on, I picked up on the heat between you two. He's more than a client."

Blake shrugged. "No, a client."

"He's gorgeous, cop or not," Colin said.

"He is gorgeous, isn't he?" Blake smiled.

"Hell, yeah. But he is not the right man to fall for, honey. He's a bad boy, dangerous. Those kind, they will break your heart and stomp all over it. Bet he's great in bed."

Blake narrowed his eyes. That was one passionate declaration, a little too much. "You got the hots for him, too, or what?"

"No, no, just saying. So, is it serious?" Colin went to sit on the sofa.

Blake shrugged. He'd have to get ready for work soon. "You asked me that already. Let's drop it, okay. It's just sex, you know."

"But great sex, I'm sure. Why don't you tell me about it? I'd like the details." Colin licked his lips. "I have to live vicariously through someone. I don't have no big, hunky cop banging down my door."

Blake went to stand. "Some other time. I really need to get ready."

Colin nodded. "I'll come down to the club today, put some paper in that G string, okay?"

"Thanks," he said. His cell phone rang. He reached for it.

Colin grabbed it.

"Hey," Blake said, annoyed. "Give me my phone, Colin. Come on."

Colin handed it to him. "Sorry, just being helpful."

Blake put the phone to his ear and walked into the kitchen. "Jackson?"

"Yeah. What's up?"

"You got my message."

"You sound weird. Someone there with you?"

Traffic sounded.

"Yes."

"I'm on my way. I'll drive you to work. Who is it? Another client?"

"No, just Colin. See you soon." He hung up.

When he turned around, the living room was empty. Colin was gone.

Blake jumped into the shower. He wasn't sure what he was going to tell Jackson. Manny had told him he didn't want him seeing Jackson anymore. Blake resented that. Manny had no right telling him who he could see or not. And Blake had the distinct feeling that Manny had been watching him, knew his every damn move.

When the doorbell rang, Blake had already pulled on a pair of ripped jeans and a black t-shirt. He hurried to the door and looked through the peephole. Jackson. He opened the door. "Hi."

"Hello," he said, walking in and closing the door. "You

said Manny was here. What time was that?"

Right to the point. A kiss would have been nice. Oh well. "Around three." Blake eyed the gun peeking out of his holster.

"What did he say exactly?" Jackson shrugged out of his coat and threw it on the sofa.

"He said that he knew you were coming around. He wanted to know where we met, what questions you were asking me. He told me you wanted information and to stay away from you."

"What did you tell him?"

"I pretended I didn't know your real name, played innocent about you being a cop. He knew I was lying." Blake reached out and handled the badge hanging around Jackson's neck. "What does DET period, SGT period, mean?"

"Detective, Sergeant."

"Then you are up there in the ranking." Blake smiled, tracing his name, Jackson Blue, with his finger.

"Not really," he said, smiling. "I'd like to be a lieutenant one day. That's my goal."

"Not a captain?"

"Naw, too much time at a desk." He met his gaze. "When Manny was here, you felt threatened?" Jackson asked, moving away. "Did he actually threaten you in words, say he'd hurt you or kill you?"

"Not directly, no. I assured him I was loyal." Blake sighed. "He said I'd better be, because if I wasn't, he wasn't sure what he'd be capable of."

"That sounds like a threat to me," Jackson acknowledged.

"And then something about how he'd be upset if something was to happen to me. It was creepy, Jackson. I think he's been watching me all the time."

Jackson nodded and sat on the sofa.

"I guess you were right," Blake said softly. "Manny will

never completely let go of me. Thanks for not saying I told you so."

Jackson was checking his phone. "Sorry," he said, "I have to make a call. I was taking a second look at a crime scene when I got your message. We'll lose the light soon." He stood and walked toward the door.

"I'll finish getting ready."

Jackson had the phone to his ear. He opened the door and walked into the hallway.

# CHAPTER FIVE

Jackson called April. She was still at the crime scene. "What's up? Uncover anything new?" he asked.

"Forensics didn't miss much," she told him. "What happened to you anyway? Where in the hell are you?"

"Not far. Did you track down that security guard again?"

"Yes, I think he drinks. He seemed out of it. Should we haul him back in?"

"Might be a good idea. At this stage, let's exhaust everything we got. I'll see you later at the precinct."

"So, ah, where are you exactly?" she asked him. "Am I going to get an answer? What was the emergency? You drove away from here like your tail was on fire."

"Taking care of some things. I'll tell you about it later. Ciao." Jackson put his phone back into his pocket, closed his eyes, and leaned against the wall in the hallway. Blake's call had worried him, stressed him out. He didn't want a repeat of Tyler.

He walked back into the apartment. Blake was standing in front of the window, looking out. This time Jackson would do things right, follow his instincts.

Blake glanced at him over his shoulder. "Everything all right?"

"No, everything sucks, but that's life."

"This winter seems endless. Here we are in March, and there is still snow on the ground."

"Pack a bag," Jackson told him.

Blake turned around, his eyes widening. "Why? Am I going somewhere?"

"Yes. You're coming to stay with me."

Blake didn't speak. His jaw slackened.

"Close your mouth. I'm not proposing marriage," he said gruffly. "You need protection, and I can't go through the official channels because what I'm doing is off the grid."

"You really think Manny would hurt me?"

"Yes, I do think that." Jackson's gaze strayed to the glass of liquor on the table. "Did you pour me a drink while I was in the hall? I'm still on duty, you know."

"No. Colin was here earlier, and he insisted on pouring me a drink." Blake laughed. "Guess he thought I was stressed out. He's a mother hen."

"Colin?" Jackson walked over to the coffee table. "That geeky guy I saw earlier?"

"Yeah. Not nice, Jackson," Blake scolded him. "Not everyone can look like you."

"Your boyfriend," Jackson murmured.

Blake laughed. "Not my boyfriend. I just said that to get a rise out of you. He's a friend. He worries about me."

"Um, so you said. How often does he come around here?"

"You jealous?"

"No, not jealous. I just find him strange, that's all." He glanced at Blake. "Where does he come from?"

"I don't know." Blake shrugged. "He never said. He talks like a New Yorker."

"What does he do for a living? Does he live alone?"

"Yeah, I guess. I think he told me he works from home. He's lonely, not the kind of guy who has 'em lined up, you know. Why the third degree?"

"You ever been to his apartment?" Jackson asked.

"Jackson, damn it, what's with you?" Blake demanded, laughing. "Stop it. I'm not sleeping with him. Don't worry."

"Have you ever been to his apartment?" Jackson asked

again, meeting his gaze.

"No. He always comes here."

"What apartment does he live in?"

"Why? Don't go harassing him now. He's the nervous type."

"I'm not going to harass him. I just want to know what apartment he lives in." Jackson took a pair of disposable plastic gloves that he had tucked in the pocket of his jacket and picked up the glass. He sniffed it.

"Now you're making me nervous," Blake announced.

"So, what apartment?"

"Three O six, I think."

"Do you have a baggie?"

"Why? Where are you taking my glass?"

"Just get me one." He took the glass to the sink and poured ninety percent of the liquor down the drain. The lab only needed a drop.

Blake handed him a plastic ziplock bag.

Jackson looked at him. "What color eyes does Jack have?"

"I don't remember. Brown. I think, can't be sure."

"Colin? What color is his eyes?"

"Blue. He's got blue eyes."

"Didn't you tell me Jack wore glasses?" Jackson slipped the glass into the bag.

"Yes. He did."

"Um. Does Colin wear contact lenses?"

"I don't know. Maybe."

"Ever seen him with glasses on?"

"No."

"Wait here. Lock the door, and don't let anyone in until you hear my voice, okay?" Jackson glanced at him.

"You are freaking me out. Where are you going?" Blake followed him to the door.

"Just pack your clothes, enough for a few days. I will

come by and get more for you if you need them." He opened the door, glanced at him. "Lock it."

He waited until he heard Blake lock the door then took the fire stairs down to the third floor.

Apartment three hundred and six was right at the end of the hallway. He approached it cautiously, hand near his gun holster. When a door opened, he whirled around to see an elderly gentleman with a small bag of what Jackson assumed was garbage.

"Hello there, young fellow," he said. Then his gaze went to the gun.

Jackson showed him the badge. "NYPD."

"Oh, okay." He smiled. "Everyone has a gun these days. Are you thinking about renting? Be nice to have a police officer next door."

"You mean *this* apartment?" Jackson hooked his thumb toward it.

"Yes. It's been empty for some time."

Jackson turned to stare at the door, then he looked back at the man. "Do you remember who lived here before?"

"A young fellow, on his own. Never had any furniture. Wasn't what I would call the friendly sort, kept to himself most of the time."

Jackson nodded. "Do you know if the concierge is in the building?"

"His office is in the lobby. You might catch him. He's Mr. Albertson. Kind of lackadaisical. My faucet in the bathroom has been dripping for months. Still hasn't fixed it."

Jackson smiled. "If you like, I'll take the garbage down with me."

"Thank you, young man. That's so nice of you. The container is right outside the main door."

Jackson took the bag from him and went down to the lobby. He deposited the garbage in the bin then came back inside and knocked on the office door.

The man, in a white undershirt, was a bald fellow with a mustache, and he had a fat sandwich in his hand when he opened the door. He looked surprised when Jackson flashed his badge. "I was just about to pay that traffic ticket." He held up a hand, almost dropping his sandwich.

"It's not here about a traffic ticket. I'd like you to show me apartment three hundred and six."

"Are you thinking about renting?" He turned and put his sandwich on the chair.

"No. I'm interested in the guy who lived there before."

"A freak," he said, locking up the office and walking to the elevator.

"What would make you say that?"

"Never had any furniture, and neighbors complained that he chanted all night. Was into some kind of devil worship."

They stepped onto the elevator. "Devil worship?"

"Yep, so they said."

"Who complained?"

"Mr. and Mrs. Burns in three O five."

"Was he evicted?"

"No." Jackson followed the concierge off the elevator. "He just up and left. Skipped on his lease."

"What name was the lease in?" Jackson followed him to the apartment and waited while the man found the key.

"Jack Colins," he said.

Jackson took a breath. "I see. Not Colin, as a first name?"

"No. Don't know anything about a Colin, said his name was Jack."

He was using an alias. "Can you describe him?"

"Blond, skinny guy, in his twenties." The concierge opened the door and let Jackson walk in.

"Did he rent a parking space? Does he drive a vehicle of some kind?"

"Never saw one," the man said.

Jackson walked into an empty apartment. He wandered through the rooms. Nothing. He took out his phone and dialed. "This is sergeant Jackson Blue. I need a APB on a Jack Colins." Jackson rattled off the address of the building and the apartment number, then gave a physical description. "This is his last known address," he said. "He was last seen at this location early today. He's to be considered dangerous. Possible suspect in ongoing murder investigation. I am to be informed as soon as suspect is located."

The man beside him looked startled. "Murder? Did he kill somebody?"

"We don't know," Jackson said, sending April a text.

Meet me at my house in an hour. I'll explain later. Bring a uniform with you.

"Thank you," Jackson told the man, putting his phone away. "You've been very helpful. Please stay in the city. We may need to ask you a few more questions. Are the neighbor's home?" He looked at the apartment three O five.

"Mr. and Mrs. Burns are away until Monday. On holiday. Their granddaughter just had a baby boy."

"Okay." Jackson handed him his card. "Have them call me as soon as they get back, okay?"

"Yes, sir," he said as he read the card. "Sergeant, eh? That's high ranking. I thought of joining the force once, becoming one of your boys in blue."

Jackson smiled and bid him a good day, taking the stairs back upstairs to Blake's apartment. He knocked at the door, waited.

"Jackson?" Blake asked.

"Yeah, open up," he said.

Blake opened the door.

"Are you ready?" Jackson walked inside.

"Yes, I'm ready but I'm still perplexed," Blake said. "When are you going to tell me what's going on?"

"I'll explain later. Get your stuff. Let's go," Jackson told him.

When they were in the car, Jackson knew Blake was going to bombard him with questions, and that was perfectly normal. Jackson pulled away from the curb, wondering how he was going to tell Blake how close he may have come to being dead tonight.

"So, come on," Blake urged. "What's happening?"

Jackson stopped at the stop sign then hung a left. Before he could answer, Blake exclaimed, "You are going the wrong way. What are you doing, Jackson? I'm going to be late for work."

"You won't be going to work," he said.

"You going to pay my bills?"

"No, but until I know exactly what is going on here, you will be under protective custody."

Blake exploded. "This is not fuckin' happening. You can't do this. I have to agree. This is kidnapping. Isn't this kidnapping?" he demanded.

Jackson glanced at him. "Maybe. I don't give a shit."

"Maybe?"

"And I'm going to need you to make a formal complaint against Manny Celino."

"No, I can't," Blake said. "Don't make me do that, Blake, okay? Why?"

"Because I need to haul his ass into the station tonight to interrogate him, and you're going to provide me with a reason."

"Damn it, Jackson. He was just talking. He was—"

Jackson turned the corner onto a quiet street in front of a park. He pulled to a stop and looked at him. "Listen to me. I think Jack Colins, or whatever his name really is, is Manny's son."

"Colin is Jack?" Blake looked confused.

"He signed the lease as Jack Colins. Was Colins his mother's name?"

Blake shook his head. "I don't know. Why wouldn't he tell me who he was?"

"I have a crazy theory in my head right now that might be pure fiction," Jackson told him. "It may all turn to shit, but I have to see it through. Until I do, I need to keep you safe, Blake. Please, let me do that."

"You're really starting to make my life hell," Blake said. "You doing this because you truly care or because you're a cop who feels guilty you couldn't save Tyler?

Jackson gripped the wheel a little harder. "Let's not go there, okay?"

"Right, you're not the one whose life is fucked up right now."

"Listen," Jackson snapped. "You can hate me or not. I don't give a fuck. But it won't change a damn thing."

Jackson turned onto his street. April's car sat outside his apartment. There was a patrol car parked behind it.

"Oh my God," Blake said. "More of you?"

"Just get out of car," Jackson instructed.

"I hate cops," Blake muttered.

April came to greet them. "Hey," she said.

"Hey," Jackson said. He glanced at Blake. "Blake Wellington, this is my partner, Detective Grant."

"You have my sympathies," Blake muttered.

April grinned at Jackson. "A fan he is not." She shook Blake's hand. "Nice to meet you, Blake. Call me April. He's been giving you a hard time, has he?"

Blake rolled his eyes. "Yes. I could lose my job because of this."

"Better than losing your life," Jackson snapped, walking over to talk to the uniform.

"You don't respect me," Blake called out.

"Take him inside, April," Jackson barked. "And, Blake, stop being such a goddamned drama queen. Jesus Christ."

April led Blake inside, opening the door with her spare key, trying to console Blake. He shook his head. The Ball and Chain wasn't the only strip club in the big Apple. What was the big deal?

The young cop was waiting for instructions and eager to carry them out. "So, stick to him like glue," Jackson told the patrolman, whose name was Benjamin Howard. "Don't let him go outside, and keep him away from the windows. I don't want him calling or texting anyone either, no internet."

"Yes, sir," he said.

They walked inside together. "He was threatened this afternoon," Jackson informed him. "He is making a formal complaint, and I want it on record as soon as possible. Take a screenshot and send it to me on my phone as soon as it's done."

"Yes, sir."

"I never agreed to that," Blake announced, overhearing Jackson's instruction.

"Give me your phone." Jackson held out his hand to Blake.

"My phone? I most certainly will not," Blake replied. "What do you want my phone for?"

"I'm confiscating it as evidence," Jackson told him.

"Like hell you are!"

April nudged the officer. "Let's ah . . . take a walk outside."

The door opened and closed.

Blake was on his feet. "You can't make me say anything about Manny. And I need my phone. I need to text the manager at the club and tell him—"

"No, don't tell him anything. You didn't call yet, did you?"

"No. I was about to when—"

"And stop being so goddamned protective of Manny. He's not your friend. Now, give me the phone, Blake." Jackson came closer. "Or I'll take it by force."

Blake put his hand in his pocket and took it out. He glared at him. "I used to like you."

Jackson took the phone. "You are like the goddamned wind. You like me, you don't, you hate me, or you want to fuck me. I'm getting used to the chaos that is in your head. Listen, I need you to help me. Just tell the officer what you told me. It won't get Manny arrested, but it will let me pick him up for questioning."

"What aren't you telling me?" Blake met his gaze.

"I'll tell you when I'm sure, okay?" Jackson reached out to touch his shoulder.

Blake pushed his hand away.

Jackson sighed and walked outside again. He nodded at the officer who went back inside. "We'll take your car," he told April.

April got behind the wheel, waiting until Jackson got into the passenger seat.

"He feels like you betrayed him," April said, starting the engine. "Just how close did you two get?"

"Closer than I intended," Jackson replied.

"He's a cutie."

"Um, yeah, he's a cute pain in the ass—in my ass especially."

She laughed. "He got to you."

Jackson sighed.

"He made you feel something," April accused. "The first time since Rob I've seen you like this. Are you in love with him?"

Jackson's eyes bulged. "Love? God, no. This guy can't even decide if he hates my guts or not."

"You could be in love with him, given time, the right circumstances." April pulled out of the parking lot.

"Right circumstances?" Jackson shook his head. "Get real."

"There is this intense sexual heat between you. I felt it in there, in spite of how angry he is."

Jackson decided he didn't like where this was going. "Drop it, okay? My feelings are all tangled up. It's my fault. I let things get out of hand."

April reached over and squeezed his hand. "You mind telling me where we're going?"

"To a strip club called the Ball and Chain. I'll give you directions. Keep going straight," he said.

"So, what's going on in that head of yours?" April asked.

"Manny Celino had a son. He calls himself Jack, but I'm sure that's because of Manny. A sick joke."

"Manny again? Jackson . . ."

"Hear me out." Jackson told her everything about this Colins guy, how he was sure that lab results would show Blake's drink had been drugged, most likely with the same drug of the last two victims.

April let out an audible gasp. "So, he was hiding his identity from Blake, and you think he was going to kill him? Why, because of you?"

"Maybe. Or he'd developed an attachment to Blake, got jealous when he saw me there. I'm thinking that somehow this is connected to Tyler's murder, too. Blake said that Jack disappeared right after Tyler was murdered. Yet Blake said Manny spoke of him like he was around. I think Manny realized his son was a serial killer and he locked him up."

"Making it worse, probably," April replied. "But now,

he's let him loose, using him for his own gain?"

Jackson shrugged. "Could be."

"He's letting his son do his dirty work," April said. "What a bastard."

"I don't think Manny could kill Blake. I do think he cares for him in some way, but I don't think he'd have qualms about letting someone else do it."

"Do you still think Manny killed Tyler, or—" April glanced at him. "They both did, father and son, together?"

"I don't know. Turn left here," Jackson told her. "Manny was involved, but now I'm beginning to think that Colin was there with him."

They rode in silence the rest of the way. April had the address on her GPS now, so Jackson didn't need to give directions anymore. His feelings were in turmoil. He was wondering if he'd just stumbled onto the right road because of Blake. He'd always felt like Blake was the key to everything, that he would lead him to Tyler's murderer. But he hadn't expected the feelings he aroused in him. The fact that Blake was angry at him bothered him, although he didn't mean to let it show. He was trying to protect him. In fact, he'd put his life on the line to protect him if he had to. It wasn't only because he was a cop. There was more, deep down, and to explore that, give in to those feelings, was preposterous. They'd known each other for such a short time. Blake was the last person he should take on as a full-time lover. They had nothing in common, except sex, and great sex it was, but Jackson wasn't sure how he'd cope with Blake's *career*. The stripping, well, that was one thing, but the sleeping with men for money, that he couldn't stomach. That was why, maybe Blake being angry at him was for the best, no matter how much it hurt.

The club was bustling. They both got a dirty look from the doorman when they showed their badges.

"Manny Celino," April said. "Any idea where he's at?"

Jackson scanned the room. He nudged April, motioned to her. Manny was in his usual place, right up front, with a few of his mobster friends.

When Jackson walked up to the table, the smile on his face died.

"Hello, gentlemen," he said. "I'm Detective Blue, and this is Detective Grant, NYPD." Jackson bent his head close to Manny's ear. "Now, we don't care to embarrass you, Manny, but you are going to need to come with us downtown."

"What for?" he asked, trying not to reveal how angry he was.

"I have a few questions about your son," Jackson told him. "And, oh, you threatened someone's life today."

Manny's eyes widened.

Jackson stared right into those startled eyes. "Shall we, or do we need the cuffs?"

"No, no," he said, getting up. "I'll come."

April drove. Jackson got into the back of the vehicle beside Manny.

"Ah, what in hell is this now?" Manny demanded. "If I'm under arrest, you'd better read me my rights, Blue, and then start praying you'll hold on to that pretty badge of yours."

"Another threat?" Jackson said. "And to think I was just being nice. I didn't want you to be lonely back here, Manny."

"You'd be the last person I'd want keeping me company," he snapped. "What do you want, Jackson? Really? And to think you had to stoop to fucking a common whore to do it."

Jackson's expression darkened. "Now your true colors come out. You've made Blake think he's special, that you actually care about him. What you care about is how much he tells the cops."

Manny shook his head. "Whores aren't usually

intellectuals."

"You're a despicable piece of shit. And I have a feeling your son may be, too." Jackson glanced out the window. It was another ten minutes to the station.

"Don't have a son."

"Really? So, what's the joke about him calling himself Jack? That's not his real name, is it?"

Manny smiled.

"I didn't think you were so obsessed with me, you'd name your kid after me. I'm flattered."

"Don't be," he said. "I don't have a kid."

"So, when did you figure out your kid was a serial killer? Was he there the night you killed Tyler?"

He looked out the window. "It's going to snow."

"He's going to prison," Jackson said.

Manny muttered something in audible.

"I'm waiting on lab results. He tried to drug Blake today. Your suggestion?"

"I would never hurt Blake."

Jackson checked his phone. "Oh, wow, Blake has made a complaint. This sure reads like threats to me."

"His word against mine," he said.

"Um, yeah, but," Jackson drawled, "if the lab test comes back positive, it's the timing." Jackson shook his head. "Bad, bad, timing."

"Fuck you, Blue," Manny muttered. "Fuck, fuck, fuck you."

Jackson smiled. "You wish."

A half hour later, Manny was in an interrogation room. He'd asked for a lawyer.

Lieutenant Delany came to stand beside Jackson as he stood watching Manny through the glass. "Making him stew?"

"Yeah. Miserable little worm."

"He's wiggling now," she said. "We can't hold him for long. That statement from Mr. Wellington is flimsy at best. And he's asking for a lawyer already?"

Jackson nodded. "I know. It's late, though, and he is going to have to get that dirtbag of an attorney of his out of bed."

She grinned. "I like your style, Sergeant. Oh, and the lab tests came back. It tested positive for Rohypnol."

"The date rape drug, the same drug that was found in the bloodstream of the two murder victims." Jackson met his boss's gaze.

Delany nodded. "That's the one. I knew there was a reason I gave you your badge back."

April came around the corner at that moment. "We got some info on Manny's offspring," she said. "Real name is Colin Harper-Celino, often referred to as Jack by those who know him. She said Manny always called him that."

"Guy is warped," Jackson muttered.

"We spoke to his mother who lives in Boston. She hasn't had contact with Colin in over five years. Said, and I quote, That freak is psychotic. Lives with his father, has been with Manny since he was a teenager. The less I see of him, the better."

"Not exactly mother of the year," Jackson said. "Any word on his whereabouts?"

"Not yet," April said.

"We can count Boston out," he said. "Date rape drug was found in Blake's glass. Blake was to be his next victim," Jackson told her.

"Oh my God." April put a hand to her chest. She glanced at Manny through the glass.

"Maybe you guys should tag team this," the lieutenant suggested. "Your history with Manny may actually be a disadvantage here, Blue."

Jackson nodded.

"Let's play good cop, bad cop," April suggested with a grin.

"Guess who the bad cop will be," Jackson smirked.

April laughed. "I'd like to be the bad cop just once."

The lieutenant shook her head. "I don't care who the bad one is, get him to talk. We have a killer on the loose and we have no idea how he'll react now that you've thrown a wrench into his plans, Jackson."

"See what you can get out of him," Jackson said to April. "I'm going to check on Blake, and I'll join you in a few." Jackson walked down the hallway and called Officer Howard who was watching Blake. "Everything okay there?"

"Fine. He's watching television. Pretty quiet."

"Put him on the phone," Jackson said.

There was some talking, then the officer came back on again. "He doesn't want to talk to you," he said. "Sorry, sir."

Jackson sighed. Why was Blake being so stubborn? Okay. He didn't want to talk to him, fine. At least he knew he was safe. "I'll check in later. I'll be there to relieve you in the morning."

"Thank you, sir," Officer Howard said and hung up.

Jackson watched through the class as April questioned Manny, the speaker open so he could hear them.

"So, where's your sidekick?" Manny asked her. "I'm sure he's listening. And where's my lawyer? I don't have to say a damn thing without my lawyer present, you know."

"It's late." April sat back in her chair. "Takes time."

Manny muttered something under his breath.

"So, where exactly was your son these last few months?"

"I don't have a son."

"Um, we found his birth records. The mother listed you as the father. We spoke to her just a little while ago. She said Colin was staying with you. Or is it Jack? Just why does he call himself Jack?"

He shrugged. "Jack who?"

"Were you at Blake Wellington's place earlier?"

"Yeah, so, he's my employee, dances at the Ball and Chain. We had business."

"You usually threaten your employees?" April asked him.

"He's hypersensitive, that boy. I wouldn't hurt a hair on his head."

"How come your son was hanging out with Blake, living in the same building with no furniture?"

"I don't know who you are talking about, Detective."

Jackson chose that moment to walk in. "Hello, Manny."

"Here we go." Manny rolled his eyes. "Going to beat me with a phonebook?"

"You've been watching too many old movies. We don't use phone books anymore." Jackson took a seat. He eyed him. "Your son may be a killer. In fact, he tried to drug Blake Wellington earlier today. Did you tell him to kill Blake?"

"He what?" Manny blinked. "He tried to kill Blake?"

"Then you do know him." April smiled.

"We found a glass laced with the date rape drug. Blake called me and didn't drink it, but if he had of, where do you think he would have ended up?" Jackson leaned closer. "Did you kill Tyler or did Colin?"

"I want my lawyer."

Jackson looked at April. "Get us some coffee, will you?"

"No way am I leaving you alone with him," she said. "And I'm not your waitress," April scoffed.

Oh, she was good. "Five minutes."

Manny shook his head. "Don't trust him," Manny told her. "He put me in the hospital once."

"Yeah, and you never bothered showing up in court," Jackson said. "Did that have something to do with your son?"

Manny appeared to panic. "Please, don't leave me alone with him," he pleaded, his gaze on April.

Jackson was impressed. He never thought Manny was that terrified of him.

"It won't hurt, five minutes," April said, getting to her feet.

"No, listen, wait until my lawyer gets here, and I'll talk about Colin, about my son."

There, Manny had said it. Jackson stood. He walked out of the room. April followed.

In the hallway, April said, "Progress. He's admitted this guy is his son."

"Yeah, but he's just telling us what we already know. He isn't giving us anything as to where that bastard would go. I'm sure he knows," Jackson told her.

April sighed. "Let's get back in there."

Jackson stayed quiet as April played the perfectly polite detective, but Manny kept glancing at him with expectation, waiting for the other shoe to drop. He was well seasoned, having been hauled in for questioning often enough.

Jackson suddenly leaned across the table, his face close to Manny's. "Do you know how many years conspiracy to murder will get you, Manny?"

He went back in his chair. "I am not a conspirator to anything."

"Hiding a serial killer kind of is." Jackson gave him an ironic smile. "The fact that he is your son doesn't give you a pass."

"Colin isn't a killer." Anger laced his voice now. "He's a little different, that's all."

"Yeah," April said, "different." She pushed the crime photos of the two victims at him. "Different did this? And we think there could be more. We're tracing his whereabouts over the last few years, have been in touch with Interpol.

Seems like his difference started awhile back."

"Perhaps with Tyler?" Jackson sneered.

"You were obsessed with that boy," Manny accused. He grinned. "Was he a good fuck, Jackson, as good a Blake?"

Jackson jumped from his seat, practically flying across the table. He had Manny by the throat.

April was saying his name. "No, Jackson, stop. Stop."

Jackson released Manny, his chest heaving. "You piece of—" He backed off. "I never laid a hand on Tyler. Unlike you, little boys don't do it for me." He doubled his fists. How he wanted to wipe that look off his face.

April had his arm. "Take a walk," she said. "Jackson, take a walk."

# CHAPTER SIX

When Blake heard the car pull up in the driveway, it was after seven in the morning. He hadn't slept all night. Instead, he'd been ruminating, thinking about how he was being kept here, babysat by a police officer. Deep down under the anger was fear. He'd always reacted like that. He'd push the fear away and let the anger surface. But this time, the fear was being overshadowed by something else, something that hurt. He didn't even want to deal with that.

He felt like he was a criminal, his phone taken away. This fueled the resentment. He focused on that.

A key in the door. The policeman greeted Jackson. "Good morning, Sergeant," he said.

Jackson said hello and looked over at Blake, who pretended to be concentrating on some morning cartoon.

Jackson was speaking low to the officer, then they said their goodbyes. The door closed. He toed off his boots and removed his coat, pushing that precious lock of hair off his forehead. "So, why didn't you talk to me last night?" he asked, walking over to the kitchen counter and removing his gun from its holster.

"I had nothing to say to you, and don't have anything to say to you now." It sounded childish, even to Blake.

Jackson took care of his gun and put a bottle of liquor out on the counter. He poured himself a tall drink and took a few swallows. "I see," he said.

Blake turned his head to watch him. "You used me from day one."

Jackson put down the drink. "I asked for your help. Where did the using come into it?"

"You used sex to keep me close to you. Don't say you didn't, Jackson."

"I can't say the thought didn't cross my mind, but you made the first move, remember? And we already had this discussion, and I really don't feel like having it again."

"Who is the real whore here?"

Jackson's mood darkened. "Jesus, that line is getting old. You already called me a whore. Fine, I'm a whore." He poured a little more in the glass.

"I didn't want to get involved with all this, or with you." Blake stood. "I was fine before you came along."

"Really? Fine? Well, maybe you were fine, Blake. But right now, you'd most likely be dead if I hadn't come along."

Blake shook his head. "What are you talking about?"

"The results came back from the lab. That drink on your coffee table was drugged. He put Rohypnol in your drink yesterday."

"What is Rohypnol?"

"Commonly known as the date rape drug." Jackson drained his glass.

"Oh my God, but why would he do that?"

"Because we think Colin is a serial killer."

Blake sunk down on the sofa. He was shaking.

"Manny let him loose, to watch you. He developed a crush on you. When he saw me at your apartment, that set him off. He most likely told Manny about us. I think Manny encouraged him to do what he was about to do."

"To . . . to kill me?" Blake was in shock.

"Yes. Kill you. Colin drugged his other victims, sexually tortured them, you don't want the details. He'd strangle them and tie an anchor to their leg before dumping them in the Hudson. His victims were male prostitutes. He'd get to know them, develop an attachment, then kill them. At least that's what our task force has been able to figure out. There have been others, and there will be more."

Blake shook his head. "Oh my God."

Jackson walked over and stood in front of him. "That night of the party. You said Manny came to get Tyler and he left you there, right?"

"Yeah. Are we going to go through that night again?"

"Yes, we are, again and again, as much as it takes. Do you remember seeing Colin, or Manny mentioning him, before or after that party? Think, Blake. Damn it."

Blake closed his eyes. That night had been a bad one. The johns had been drunk and none too gentle. Blake had felt humiliated and scared. He'd wanted it to all be over. An image of Manny came to his mind. He saw him as he'd walked into the suite. He'd been agitated.

"I was happy to see him," Blake told Jackson. "I thought he'd come to take us all out of there. I remember him pushing me aside and pulling Tyler toward the door. The door to the suite was open and—" Blake took a breath.

"And?"

"There was someone with Manny, waiting at the door, hovering there."

"Colin," Jackson said. "Manny brought Colin with him to the suite that night."

Blake nodded. "Maybe, I didn't see him clearly."

"Did Manny know you saw Colin?"

"I . . . I think so," Blake said, trying to remember. "I was moving to the door. I guess I thought I could talk Manny into letting me come, too. I saw a face peering around the corner. He knows I saw him. Manny probably thinks I knew who it was, but I didn't. I didn't get a good enough look at him, Jackson."

"Manny doesn't know that, Blake. He's never known for

sure and that's why he's keeps you close to him but hasn't killed you. When Colin told him I was there, Manny knew you were talking to me. He got scared. Colin got jealous. Manny told Colin to drug you, bring you to him, or just do what he does — kill you."

"Do you really think Manny told him to kill me?" Blake was in a state of disbelief.

"I don't know. We won't know until we find Colin. I'm going to get some sleep and go back to work. We had to release Manny, and in spite of his promise to tell us everything, all we know was that Colin is his son. He claims he has no idea where Colin is, but I'm not sure about that. We got people keeping a close watch on Manny, and an all-points bulletin on Colin."

"He's probably a million miles away," Blake said.

Jackson shook his head. "No. Usually they hide in plain sight, just like he was doing living in your building."

"Jackson, you can't go to sleep," Blake told him. "What if he comes here?"

"Don't worry, there is a squad car outside."

"Oh, okay." Blake swallowed.

"I thought you hated cops?" Jackson eyed him. "It's funny how people hate us until they need us for something."

"You saved my life. I've been an asshole." Tears filled his eyes.

Jackson walked back to the kitchen. "Don't worry about it. Coffee? I'll make some."

"Sounds good."

They didn't talk much after that, each with their own thoughts. Blake was thinking about his life, what it had been, and what he wanted it to be. If he lost his job, he'd find another, but he'd probably have to give up the apartment, settle for a room somewhere. The dream of Manny paying for his education was finished now, not that it was ever going to happen. He'd been naïve, but it was all he'd had. Now, the dreams were dead. He had nothing.

Blake glanced at Jackson sitting in the recliner opposite him. How handsome and sexy that man was. It was unreal how much need Jackson aroused in him, but he had to come back to earth now. A man like that was never going to want to be with a guy like him. They were too different. He could never be worthy of someone like that, a cop, a hero, a decent man. He smiled. Jackson's eyes had closed. He'd fallen asleep in the chair. Blake wanted to touch him, but he didn't. Instead, he took the blanket off the sofa and put it over Jackson, looking down at him. If only things had been different in his life. If he'd met Jackson in another place, maybe.

Blake was surprised when he returned to the sofa that there were tears in his eyes again. He was scared but had never been prone to crying. Colin was still out there. He'd tried to kill him. He could try again.

"Are you okay?" Jackson's eyes were open.

"I'm okay," Blake said. "You fell asleep."

"Yeah, I'm beat," he said. "I think I'll go to bed for a few hours then get back to the station."

"You're leaving again then," Blake said, meeting his gaze. He tried to keep his voice from shaking. He just felt safer with Jackson there.

Jackson stood. "There's room in the bed for two."

Blake widened his eyes, but he didn't question it. He just followed Jackson into the bedroom.

Jackson pulled off his t-shirt and undid his jeans.

Blake swallowed hard, trying not to become hypnotized by the sight of the man's hard, well-muscled chest. He tore his gaze away from him and crawled into bed, leaving on his clothes.

Jackson glanced at him. "You going to sleep in your clothes?"

"Yeah," he said.

Jackson didn't pursue the topic. He got into bed beside him and turned away, onto his side. "Sleep well," he said.

Blake sucked in some air. There was too much space between them, but that was how it had to be now. Blake closed his eyes. No. This was torture. Why in the hell did he want him so badly? Blake turned onto his side as well, clinging to the end of the bed. He prayed for sleep to take this ache inside him away. *Jackson.* His cock was stiffening by the minute. *Damn it. Damn it.* Jackson had gone to sleep.

Blake rolled over again and moved closer to him. He slipped his arm over Jackson's waist and rested his cheek on his back. Seconds later, Jackson's hand covered his, squeezed it. "It's okay now," Jackson told him softly. "Sleep, Blake."

When Blake opened his eyes, he was alone in the bed. The sun was streaming through the window, and Jackson was talking to someone. Blake glanced at the pillow where Jackson's head had lain, and brought it closer, putting it under his own head. He breathed in his scent and closed his eyes.

Jackson's voice grew louder. Blake sighed and got out of bed. The clock on the nightstand told him it was a little after three in the afternoon. He walked out into the hallway rubbing his eyes.

Jackson was on the phone. "There are four vehicles registered in Celino's name," Jackson explained. "I want all those vehicles accounted for, every single one. Get a squad car over there now. I want each one photographed and verified. If there is one missing, I want to know." He paused. "No, get a damn warrant if you need one."

Jackson marched around, phone in hand. He had showered, had put on jeans and a blue shirt, sleeves rolled up. His gun was holstered across his shoulder. That meant he'd be leaving him again.

"There are no cars registered to Colin Harper-Celino?" Jackson sounded unconvinced. Well, check again. He has a driver's license. Check his insurance records, too. If he has so much as a traffic ticket, I want to know. I'll be there soon." He hung up.

Blake smiled at him. "Hey."

"Hey. I made fresh coffee. It's on the table, and I ran out to get some food," Jackson said, all the while checking his phone. "You should be okay."

"You want me to make you something?" Blake watched him as Jackson picked up his coat.

"No, I gotta go. I'm just waiting on the—"

"Babysitter," Blake supplied.

"Yeah." Jackson grinned at him. "Babysitter."

A dedicated cop, highly charged, so focused on getting his suspect, Blake knew Jackson wouldn't rest until he did.

The cop arrived, a woman this time. Her name was Officer Nancy Wright. Jackson spoke to her for a few minutes then headed to the door. He glanced back at Blake for a second. "Stay put. I'll be back later."

"Jackson," Blake said, coming closer. He paused then said, "Be careful, okay?"

Jackson nodded and left.

The officer locked the door behind him. She turned around and smiled at Blake. "So, what would you like to do? You play cards?"

Blake sighed. "Sure. I'm going to shower and get dressed, have some breakfast. Later, okay?"

She nodded. "Take your time."

Blake was bored. It had only been two days, but the time seemed to go by so slowly. He couldn't call anyone. There was always the same old crap on television. The police officers had been nice enough, but cops weren't his favorite people.

In the shower, Blake was thinking about all the cops he'd encountered in his life. Some of them just loved to come down to Times Square and harass the prostitutes. They'd haul you in just for standing in the wrong place. There were others who made you suck them off in the patrol car if you didn't want to spend the night in a jail cell. The good ones were few and far between.

Blake turned off the shower and wrapped himself in a towel. He walked into Jackson's bedroom and sat on the bed. Jackson had put his overnight bag in the corner, and he'd let him sleep beside him in the bed. Blake wasn't sure what that meant. Was he going to be allowed to sleep here with him again? Part of him didn't want to. It had been hard to sleep in his bed and not touch him, but then there was the frightened part of him that felt safe feeling him there beside him.

Blake lay back on the bed, closed his eyes. He remembered the room he'd had as a kid. His mother had decorated it with shiny little planets and spaceships. There were stars on the ceiling. He'd been a happy child, loved and cherished. His mother had raised him alone, working two part-time jobs, one as a bank teller, and the other as a piano teacher. She'd never told him who his father was. And Blake had never asked. It just didn't seem that important.

Then one day when Blake was only eleven years old, the bank where his mother worked was robbed. She was shot and killed. Blake would never forget the day he'd been called to the principal's office. There was a strange lady there with blonde hair, carrying a briefcase. They'd told him his mother was dead and that child services would place him with a foster family. There was no one who would take on the responsibility of an eleven- year-old boy.

Tears. Blake remembered crying so many tears that eventually there'd been none left. The children's home was cold, and the children were mean, and Blake couldn't fathom how he would go on without his mother.

Then he was sent to live with a foster family. It was the summer he'd turned twelve. He remembered how the social worker had told him that everything would be all right. He'd have a family again. Initially, he'd been happy to leave the children's home. It was a couple in their thirties, Marcia and Kenneth Pettigrew. They lived on a farm. From the moment he'd arrived, they'd put him to work, feeding chickens and raking muck. Two weeks later, Marcia and Kenneth Pettigrew walked into his room in the middle of the night and forced Blake to have sex with each of them, while the other one watched and took pictures.

The first chance Blake had, he ran away, walking miles, hitchhiking, until he made it back to the city. He didn't know how to survive on the street. He had no money, and it was autumn. It was cold on the streets at nights. That was when he'd met Manny. Scared, alone, hungry, Blake would have accepted help from the Devil at that time. Maybe Manny was the Devil. Manny had taken care of him, but there was a price. He promised Blake he'd protect him. He had. He'd made sure he had a roof over his head and food in his stomach. The drugs helped him lose his inhibitions. High, he could do just about anything the customer wanted.

Then Tyler was murdered, and Manny whisked him away to Italy. He'd been so nice to him there. Blake hadn't had to work. He'd just enjoyed the sun and relaxed. The subject of Jack, now known as Colin, came up occasionally. Blake was never sure if Manny was his father or not. Now, it seemed as if Manny was protecting a serial killer and that Jack or Colin was his son.

What had made Blake think he could just walk away from this life unscathed? Why had he been so naïve to think that Manny really cared about him when all this time, he'd been using him, like he did with all the others?

Then there was Jackson. From the moment that cop had come into his life, he'd complicated everything. Now, Blake was trapped here, dependent on Jackson to protect him. Blake wished they'd never had sex, because now he couldn't forget about it. And he really did need to. There would never be anything more between him and Jackson, no matter how much he might fantasize that they would ride off into the sunset together.

Blake sat up. He opened the top drawer of the nightstand. Condoms, lube, cock ring, nipple clamps. He closed it again and opened the bottom drawer. He knew he shouldn't be pawing around, but boredom would do that.

In the bottom drawer was a badge, the same badge Jackson wore around his neck. Why did he have two? Then he remembered reading somewhere that cops often left the genuine badge at home and wore a copy, in case someone took it, or it got damaged.

Blake held it, running his fingers over it. Then he spotted a picture frame. It was turned upside down. Blake took it out and turned it over. It was Jackson. He looked a little younger, in a pair of shorts and a tank top, and he was leaning his chin on the shoulder of another man, who was smiling, a handsome man, older, fair hair, blue eyes. He was shirtless, in bathing trunks, nicely built. In the background was the beach and the ocean.

Blake stared at it for a long time, not sure how that picture made him feel. It shouldn't have had any effect on him at all, but it did. He felt envious, jealous even. Who was he? Was this Rob, the one Jackson had mentioned to him once? How long had they been lovers? Jackson claimed they'd broken up over Tyler's murder.

Blake replaced the picture, feeling guilty. He stood, dried off, and pulled on a pair of jeans and a t-shirt. He returned to the living room and plunked down on the sofa.

It was after midnight when Jackson finally came through the door and relieved the police officer. He toed off his boots. He had a brown paper bag in his hand. "Chinese," he said, handing the bag to a curious Blake, so he could take off his jacket.

"Smells good." Blake peeked inside, watching Jackson go through the routine with his gun in the kitchen.

"Hungry?"

"I can always eat." Blake smiled.

"Get two plates," he said, taking forks out of the drawer.

"Nancy made chicken," Blake told him, taking the dishes out of the cupboard, "but it seems like ages ago."

"Nancy?" Jackson raised an eyebrow. "You're getting pretty chummy with these cops. Next you'll be dating one of them."

Blake froze. He knew Jackson meant it like a joke. He looked at him. "You're a . . . cop."

"Yeah," he said, opening the little boxes of rice and chow mein, "but you're not dating me." He filled his plate and walked over to the sofa. "Take what you want."

Blake forked out some food, deep in thought. He came and sat beside him. "So, ah, what is it like to date you?"

Jackson had the folk halfway to his mouth. He put it back on his plate. "What?"

"Where would you take me on a first date?" He felt shy asking that but for some reason he really wanted to know.

Jackson shrugged. "What's this about?"

"Where did you and Rob go on your first date?"

"I'd rather not talk about Rob. How do you know about . . . Oh, yeah, I mentioned him to you once. History." He went back to eating.

"Was it really Tyler's murder that broke you up, or were there other things?" Blake waited.

"I told you, I'd rather not discuss Rob. Thanks."

"It still hurts."

Jackson swallowed. "The fact that I never nailed Manny for Tyler's murder? Yeah, it hurts like hell."

"Your feelings for Rob."

"What are you, Betty Lovelorn?"

"Who is she?"

Jackson laughed. "Never mind. I don't want to talk about my relationship with Rob, okay?"

"He was handsome, a little older but sexy."

Jackson put his plate on the coffee table. "How do you know?"

"What?"

"How do you know Rob was older?"

"You told me." Shit. How had that gotten out?

"No, I didn't." He got to his feet. "You been going through my things?" He looked pissed.

*Shit.* "No, I mean, I was trying to find something, and it was just there." Blake winced.

"You were trying to find it the drawer of my nightstand?" He put his hands on his hips. "What were you looking for?"

"What?"

"Stop stalling for time. What were you looking for there?"

"A, well, a washcloth."

"Washcloth."

He didn't believe him.

"Okay, I was snooping. I got bored."

Jackson pointed at him. "Don't do it again."

Blake nodded. "Okay. I'm sorry. Am I forgiven?"

"We'll see," Jackson muttered, walking over and putting his plate in the sink. "Going to take a shower."

Blake finished eating. He walked over to the sink and rinsed his plate. The sound of water running through the pipes came from the bathroom. There was a way to make it up to him. Blake smiled. He walked down the hallway, slipped into the bedroom, and took a condom and some lube out of the top drawer. The door to the bathroom was ajar. Was that an invitation? Probably not, but he was going to go in anyway.

Blake opened the door a little wider. His cock was already reacting, and all he could see was the steam from the shower. Blake moved his hand down to the zipper on his jeans. As he drew closer, the outline of Jackson's naked body through the foggy glass door came into view. He licked his lips and took off his jeans, tearing off his t-shirt at the same time. He took a jagged a breath, looking down at his own erection then reached out and slowly slid back the door.

Jackson's head was under the spray. He reached a hand back to push wet hair out of his face and then froze.

Blake stepped into the shower and closed the door. He put the condom and lube on the side of the tub. Jackson noticed the supplies, then their gazes met and locked. "Can I stay?" Blake traveled his gaze down over Jackson's wet flesh to his cock, already jutting out, brushing Blake's hip as he moved in closer.

Jackson didn't answer with words. Instead, he lifted Blake's chin and brought his mouth down hard on his. He pulled him out from under the water and pressed Blake's back against the cool, wet tiles. He lifted his arms, pinning them to the wall as the assault on Blake's open mouth continued. Blake gulped Jackson's kisses, loving the feeling of being held captive by him. He pushed his hips out, desperate to feel his own erection against Jackson's. Then, with one firm jerk, Jackson whirled Blake around to face the wall. He yanked his hips forward and nudged his legs farther apart.

Blake was breathing hard, his face pressed to the tiles. Jackson lifted his hands over his head. "Leave them there." He reached around and fondled Blake's erection, handled his testicles, then maneuvered his hand up to tweak each nipple hard.

Black moaned softly. "Baby. Use me," he pleaded.

Jackson fondled Blake's cock again while lubed-coated fingers snaked up inside his ass, locating his prostate. Blake let out a shout, moving back and forth on the fingers, fucking them furiously. Moaning, he let his head go back, and Jackson propelled it to the side to kiss his mouth again. As Jackson's tongue slid around Blake's, his sheathed cock pushed up hard inside him.

Jackson pulled his mouth away, pressing Blake's cheek to the wall. He grabbed Blake's hips with both hands and fucked him hard and deep, increasing the speed as he went. Flesh slapped flesh accompanied by the heavy pounding of the shower and their murmured sounds of pleasure.

"Baby, oh yeah, baby," Blake cried out as Jackson grabbed his shaft again, jerking it hard, propelling them both into the little death of orgasm.

As Blake came, Jackson pulled out, turned Blake around, and pressed him to his knees. He held out his cock to him, taking off the condom. "Suck it." Hands on Blake's head. Blake took Jackson's cock into his mouth, sucking and licking, swallowing more and more until Jackson shouted out his release, taking a step back to rest.

Blake looked up at him. Jackson's eyes were closed, his hand moving over his chest. Blake stood, got closer. He pressed his lips to his chest, exploring his biceps, forearms. *The angels must have wept creating him. He's too damn beautiful.*

Jackson wrapped his arms around him. Their lips met again, a slow, succulent, heart-stopping kissing. *This guy can kiss.*

Jackson suddenly reached over and turned off the water. He got out and threw Blake a towel, drying off himself. He held out his hand. "Come on," he said. "Come to bed."

Blake smiled. "You tired?"

"No," he whispered, "not tired at all."

That made Blake smile even more.

"Don't bother putting anything on," Jackson told him, meeting his gaze.

"Damn, I'm hard again," Blake grinned.

Jackson didn't comment. He led him out of the bathroom by the hand. In the bedroom, he told Blake to get on the bed. Blake didn't hesitate.

Jackson opened the top drawer. He threw a cock ring, nipple clamps, and a vibrating sex toy on the bed, along with lube and condoms. Finally, he took out handcuffs, the furry kind. "They don't hurt," he whispered, cuffing both wrists together, then to the bed.

Blake licked his lips, his cock springing totally to life.

"This really turns you on, doesn't it?" Jackson said.

"You turn me on," Blake replied. "No one has ever turned me on like you do."

Jackson smiled, showing Blake a feathery flogger. "Is that so?" He fluttered the flogger over Blake's cock. It tickled. Jackson wrapped his fist around Blake's cock and squeezed.

"Oh, yeah," Blake moaned.

Next, he slipped on the cock ring at the base. "Spread your thighs wide," he instructed, with just enough authority that Blake shivered all over with excitement.

Blake spread his legs.

"Um, nice, look how hard I am . . ." Jackson stroked his own cock.

Blake moved his hips in response, watching as Jackson now spread some lube on his hands. He reached over and rubbed the lube into Blake's nipples. They stiffened. Damn. His cock jerked in response. He felt so horny, so sexy. He closed his eyes, moaning softly. Jackson pinched his slippery nipple. Then he felt the nipple clamps bite into his sensitive flesh once then twice as the chain between them teased over his stomach and down to his cock where Jackson attached to the cock ring. As he moved, it tugged in both places. Yum. This was nice.

The vibrating noise began as Jackson coated a thick, ribbed sex toy with lots of lube. Blake smiled. "You going to fuck me with that?"

"For starters," he said, grabbing a pillow and pushing it under Blake's hips so his anus was accessible.

The clamps were doing their work on his nipples and cock again, and Blake groaned with pleasure.

The tip of the toy probed the opening to his ass, and his cock oozed pre-come. Jackson pushed it in just a little then used the flogger on his cock and nipples. Blake was breathing hard. Jackson reached down with his hand and pushed it another inch, flogging again.

Blake bit down on his lip. The vibrator was making his cock ache. He was glad Jackson had put it on. He didn't want to come. Not yet. This was too damn good. The light flogging on his cock and nipples, the vibrator now pushed all the way up inside his ass, had him flexing his body, which in turn pulled on the clamps. He was in heaven.

Jackson held his legs open and licked the head of Blake's cock, loosening the cock ring. He withdrew the vibrator out then shoved it back in, none too gently. Blake cried out, his cock sputtering.

The cock ring came off, the sex toy was gone, only to be replaced by Jackson's thick cock. As Jackson fucked his ass, he played with the nipple clamps, and Blake cried out his pleasure. Jackson rocked their bodies up and down, coming soon after.

A few minutes later, the handcuffs came off, and Blake gently removed the clamps, licking each nipple. Blake placed a hand on Jackson's head, caressing his hair, then pulled his head onto his shoulder.

"You're good at that," Blake said. "Do you enjoy it?"

Jackson shrugged. "You like it. I like to please."

"Oh, you do, you do." Blake laughed. "Have you ever been to a dungeon? You'd make a good Master."

Jackson laughed, too. "It's really not my scene. Is it yours?" He looked at him.

"No. What we did tonight, wow, that's as wild as I'd like to get. You are so sexy." He kissed Jackson's hair.

"You, too," Jackson admitted. He sat up. "I need to clean up."

"Me, too," Blake said.

"Ah, let me go it alone, okay?" Jackson grinned. "You are way too much of a temptation."

Blake smiled. "Okay. Nice to know." Blake watched him leave the room and closed his eyes. The shower turned on again. It was nice to pretend for a few minutes that Jackson was his. He'd come home from work, they'd eat together, make love, then fall asleep in each other's arms. Only, he had nothing to offer Jackson. What? He'd turn into some kind of a housewife, scrubbing the floors and doing his laundry.

Jackson had been in love with a man who was a police officer, like himself. He had a life. He had a job. He wasn't an unemployed loser whose claim to fame was having a few high-profile celebrities as clients. No, this couldn't last, and frankly, Blake couldn't believe that he wanted it to.

When Jackson came out of the bathroom, Blake took his turn. When he returned to bed, Jackson had fallen asleep. Blake smiled and moved close to him. Soon he, too, was asleep.

The next day, as Jackson got ready to leave, Blake wanted to tell him how he felt something more than he'd ever imagined. Was it love? He didn't know. It was something that made him want to touch him all the damn time, look into his eyes.

They ate together, bagels and cream cheese and good coffee. Jackson spent half his time on the phone, but it didn't matter. He was here, in front of him. Jackson's presence gave him comfort. When the police officer came to the door, Blake was disappointed. It meant Jackson was leaving again, and sometimes he didn't return for ten or twelve hours.

The cop's name was Kevin Nivens, and he wasn't very talkative. Blake took a book off the bookshelf in the hallway and started reading. *Techniques of Investigation* was not the most exciting book. It was more of a manual than anything, but it gave Blake an idea about the work Jackson did. There were actual cases based here in the city, a little gory but fascinating.

"What are you reading?" Mr. Personality Officer suddenly decided to be social.

Blake held up the book. "A police procedural," he said carefully. "Or something like that."

"I want to be a detective," he said, coming over and sitting in the chair opposite.

"That's great," Blake said.

"What do you do for a living?"

"Ah, I'm in recreation," he said.

"Like party planning?" he asked.

"Right, just like that. How long have you been on the force, Kevin?"

"Three months."

Blake smiled, nodded, but something knotted in his stomach. *Only three months? Oh, well, it's just babysitting.*

They didn't talk too much after that. The police officer turned on the television and watched sports. Blake dozed awhile. They ate frozen pizza, and Blake decided to go into the bedroom and look for another book. This one was getting tedious.

When he came back out, he realized that he was alone. Where the hell was that cop? "Kevin?" he called out.

"Hello, my beautiful, Blake," a voice said from behind him.

Blake turned around, widening his eyes. Colin stood there. He was covered in blood. Blake swallowed hard, trying not to show his fear. "Where is the police officer who was here a while ago?"

He smiled. "He fought a lot. If he'd cooperated, there wouldn't be such a mess on Sergeant Blue's nice carpet."

Blake's terror grew. "Jackson is on his way here, you know."

"No, he's not," Colin said. "He's going to be later than usual. He's at a murder scene, or he will be as soon as he finds one of Daddy's cars."

Blake raised a hand to his mouth. "Oh God. Why? Why, Jack?"

"I don't want to hurt you, Blake. I love you," he said softly. "Don't you know that?"

Blake inched toward the door. "Then let me go."

Colin shook his head. "Can't. You see it's Jackson we want."

"We? Who is we? And why Jackson? He didn't do anything to you." Blake glanced at the door.

"You'll never make it," Colin told him, shaking his head.

Blake ran over to the door. Colin was right behind him. He grabbed Blake's hair. Blake let out a scream, struggling to get away. He managed to run around the sofa and into the hallway. Colin caught him in front of the bathroom. Something sharp stung in his arm. He stumbled, falling to his knees in front of Jackson's bed.

A hand gripped his hair and pulled his head back. Three swirling faces looked down at him. "That's it, you're where you do your best work, Blake. On your knees. Now sleep,

sleep."

It was the movement that roused him sometime later. It was dark, and he was in a confined space. They were moving, in a vehicle. Damn it. He was in the trunk of some car. His head felt heavy. He wanted to sleep but he fought it. He banged on the lid of the trunk. "Jack. Jack. Let me out of here."

Suddenly a blast of music invaded his ears. Blake hyperventilated as the Rolling Stones belted out *Sympathy for the Devil*. Panic was setting in. "Jack, Jack, please, please."

# CHAPTER SEVEN

"Sarge, we got a report of a break-in at six-ten West Sixty-Eighth Street. And you might find this interesting. Guess what we found abandoned in the driveway?"

"What?" Jackson gripped the phone.

"A two thousand and sixteen, Audi A four, silver blue, license plate number, G A P, four, five, six, seven, the car missing from Manny Celino's vehicles."

"Fuck. We're not far. We're near the harbor," Jackson said into his phone as he started the engine. "We'll be there in ten minutes."

"This is our first break," April said, the strain showing on her face. "Damn, he's playing with us, Jackson."

"Yeah. I think you may be right. Have someone pick up Manny. Time for another little talk," Jackson told her.

"Already on it," April said, phone to her ear.

Jackson went through every red light while April was preoccupied with the phone. When he screeched to a halt outside the small duplex at the end of the street, a crowd of people were gathered around. There were about six patrol cars, an ambulance, and the medical examiner's wagon lined up out front.

The lieutenant came walking over with her notebook as soon as Jackson and April got out of the car. "We have a victim, male, late forties, Hebert Fontaine," she said, "worked nights at the docks, multiple stab wounds. Neighbor upstairs didn't hear or see anything. She was napping. She did say that Fontaine had a vehicle, and that it was usually parked in the driveway, as it was this morning. It's missing. It was a Honda Civic, red. I got someone getting us more info as we speak."

An officer hurried over to them now. "Lieutenant," he said. "We got a make on the car, registered to a Hebert Fontaine, two thousand and fourteen, license plate number P E C, four, five, six, eight. Recently was in a traffic accident, right fender is damaged."

April scribbled it down in her notebook. "Put an all-points bulletin out on that car," she told him, following Jackson, who was already heading to the building.

The lieutenant joined them as they walked inside. They all put on the crime scene gear, including the paper shoes and plastic gloves, before walking in. The forensic team were busy doing their work.

April was preparing to examine the victim, who was on the floor behind the kitchen counter. She leaned down and took the sheet off him. "He's a mess," she said, looking up at Jackson.

Jackson sighed. His gaze followed the direction of the blood trail. "He stabbed him first in the bedroom. He's only wearing underwear. It may mean they had sex or were about to."

"No sign of forced entry," April said.

"He knew him," Jackson conferred.

"Okay," the lieutenant commented. "Find out everything you can about this Fontaine guy."

"We got a time of death?" Jackson asked the lieutenant.

"Not more than a few hours," she replied.

"Ah, Sergeant Blue," one of the crime lab people, Peter Freemont, motioned to him from across the room, "you're going to want to see this."

Jackson walked over to him. "What is it?"

Peter held up a sheet of paper. "Found it in the bedroom

on the back of the door."

April and Lieutenant Delany came to check it out as well. Jackson took the paper.

"Is that written in blood?" he asked him, wrinkling his nose.

"That's my guess," Peter replied with a nod.

Jackson peered at the words then read them aloud. "Hi, Jacky Blue. How do you do? This one's for you. Wait and see what next I do. You will go, boo, hoo, hoo, unless you say, nice to see you?"

"Shit," April said softly. "He's a sick bastard."

Jackson gasped. "Blake," he said.

"What?" April asked.

"I've got to check on Blake." Jackson ran outside. "Come on, I got to get home." April was on his tail. He called the number for the police officer on duty at his house. *You have reached Officer . . .*

They jumped into the car. April drove. Blake tried the number again and again. Then he called his home phone. Nothing. "Come on, come on, pick up," he urged, wanting to smash his phone in two. Finally, he knew. "He's got Blake, April. He took Blake."

The door stood ajar. Jackson's heart sank as he got out of his car and took out his gun.

April came up beside him. "I'll check the perimeter."

"He's not here," Jackson told her as he ran toward his building. He sidled up beside the door, gun up, then quickly moved in. The first thing he noticed was that the coffee table was tipped over. A few feet away, the standing lamp was on its side, glass from the shade scattered on the carpet like tiny diamonds.

April came running in now. "I found Fontaine's vehicle," she said. "No sign of the radio car. Tire tracks on the left side of the house."

Jackson sucked in some air.

"I put an APB on the squad car." She paused, looked around. "Shit, a cyclone hit this place?"

Jackson forced his feet to move. It was then he saw the blood pooling over near the bathroom door. Jackson froze.

April put a hand on his arm. "I'll go. Stay here."

He shook his head. "No. I'm right behind you." He felt as if he were in a movie. It didn't seem real. *Blake*. God, if something happened to him, he wasn't sure what he'd do. Tyler all over. He didn't want to think about it.

"Jackson," April said as she went into the bathroom. "It's not Blake." She poked her head around the bathroom door. "It's one of ours."

His sudden sense of relief made him feel guilty. A cop was dead, a young one, but Jackson was half crazy with the thought that it could have been Blake.

Jackson carefully made his way to the bathroom, trying not to step in the blood. "Oh God," he said when he saw him. "He was twenty-one. That butcher."

"It was quick anyway," April said, tears in her eyes.

It seemed he'd slit his throat from behind while he was taking a leak. Officer Kevin Nivens probably never saw it coming.

April was on the phone to forensics. Soon Jackson's apartment would be crawling with police. He walked down the hallway again, noting the shambles of his living room. Then his home phone rang. The sound of it sent shivers down his spine. April came to stand beside him. They both stared at the phone.

Jackson reached over and picked it up. He didn't speak. He just listened.

Then came the voice, male, sounding quite warm and jubilant. "Hello, Jackson."

Jackson put the phone on speaker. "Where is Blake, you bastard? If you have hurt him, I'm going to rip you apart with my bare hands."

"Sounds fun. Have to catch me first. And what's with the attitude, handsome? Didn't your mother ever tell you that you can catch more flies with honey than vinegar?"

"Where is he?" Jackson tightened his fingers on the phone.

"If you want to see Blake again, you need to get into your car now, alone, and head toward Jersey. Wait for my call." The line went dead.

Jackson looked at April. "I've got to go. You handle things here."

"Jackson." April grabbed his arm. "Not like this. Let me call Delany. She'll bring you a wire, a tracker for the car. What if—"

"There's no time for that," he said, heading to the door. "Try not to worry."

"Worry?" April chased after him outside. "That sadistic fuck has killed at least four people, one of them a cop. I don't want you to be number five."

"He's got Blake. Listen, as soon as I know his location, I'll call you." Jackson got into the car. "I want you to question Manny, find out if his dear offspring had any hiding spots, or special getaway places, a cabin in the woods or a condo somewhere." He started the engine. "Beat it out of him if you have to."

"All right, all right. Call me," she hollered at him, turning around and throwing up her hands in frustration.

Jackson sped away, passing the forensics team and three squad cars with their sirens wailing, on the way.

He drove for what seemed like an eternity, clutching his phone, waiting for that call. Colin was playing with him, but why? What did he want? Was Blake all right? Had Colin hurt him, killed him already?

When the phone rang, Jackson was disappointed to see

April's name. "I can't talk," he told her. "In case he calls."

"Nothing?"

"No. I feel like an idiot, driving around, going no fuckin' place. And I'll lose the light soon."

"They found the squad car. He abandoned it in the Pine Barrens, just before Mt. Laurel."

"Shit. Is he on foot then?" Jackson turned around and headed toward Trenton. "He can't be, not with Blake. He must have picked up another vehicle."

"That would be my guess. We are on alert for any reports of a stolen vehicle in the area."

"Okay. He's taken Blake to Pine Barrens. Damn it. I gotta hang up."

"The lieutenant has alerted the Jersey and Philadelphia police."

"Is Manny still in custody?"

"Yeah. He's not saying much, screaming about wanting a lawyer."

"Find out if he has any property in the Barrens."

"Okay, bye." She hung up.

"Come on," Jackson said, staring at the phone. He slammed his fist on the wheel. "Call, you freak. Call!"

It was almost a half hour before the phone rang again. Jackson had just stopped to fill the tank. He took a breath and answered on the third ring. "Okay, what do you want me to do now?"

"Where are you, darling?"

"Heading to Trenton. And don't call me darling."

"Smart boy. Sensitive boy."

"Put Blake on the phone," Jackson insisted.

"He's a little tied up right now." Laughter.

Jackson swore. "I want to hear his voice or I'm turning around and going home."

Silence.

"Now!" Jackson bellowed into the phone.

A few moments later, Blake said, "Jackson, don't come here."

"Blake? Blake? Are you all right?"

Colin came back on the phone. "He's a little sleepy. Satisfied?"

"Colin, listen, we can work this out. There doesn't need to be any more bloodshed."

"That might have worked if I was Colin," he said. "You're talking to Jack now. That wimp, Colin, he's far too much of a pussy."

Jackson narrowed his eyes. "So, ah, Colin is there with you, too?"

"Somewhere hiding. I plan to end him eventually. He's never been anything but trouble to me, always scared and whimpering, pathetic. Colin is pathetic."

Split personality, that's why the two names?

"Okay," Jackson said. "Where do you want me to meet you, Jack?"

"First, I have a few questions. If you answer them honestly, then we'll meet. If you don't, I'm going to start cutting off parts of Blake."

Jackson swallowed. "I'll answer anything. What do you want to know?"

"Okay, what do you think about when you fuck?"

Jackson narrowed his eyes. *Okay . . .*"Ah, nothing, fucking," he said. "Getting off. Next question?"

"Did you love Tyler?"

"Love him?"

"Were you in love with Tyler?"

The question shocked him. Tyler was a child. "Of course not," he snapped. "He was just a baby."

"He used to cry in my arms. Did you know that?"

"No, I didn't know that."

"He told me you were coming to take him away, and one day you'd be together forever."

Jackson sighed. "Tyler was a boy, a child," he repeated. He was aware that Tyler had developed a crush on him. He hadn't paid too much attention to it.

"But you promised him that you'd be his lover, didn't you?"

"No, I never promised him that. I told him he was too young for me. He was a boy."

"So, did you sleep with him or not?"

"No, goddamn it." Jackson was losing his temper. "I don't sleep with kids. Did he tell you that I slept with him?"

"No. But Tyler wanted you quite badly. He told me. So sweet, he was. I loved him, too. If it hadn't of been for you, he might have loved me back. You could have saved both of us, Jackson."

"I would have saved you, if I'd known about you."

"Tyler must have mentioned me."

"No. He didn't, not really."

Silence. Then he said, "He didn't want to make you jealous."

"I guess so. Why did you kill Tyler? You said you loved him."

"I didn't mean to tell Daddy about you and him. You were lying to him, Jackson, using your good looks to seduce him, make him say things, just like you are doing with Blake. Daddy meant to scare him, make him stop talking to you, but Tyler loved you so much. He said he wouldn't stop seeing you, never. He said he'd rather die. He never loved me, even when Jack came along, so like you, tough and macho. He is you."

"Who is me?" Jackson asked. "Jack is me?"

"Yes, he is you, only he's mean." There was some whimpering.

"Colin?" Jackson asked.

"Blake never loved me either. You seduced him. You have been fucking him. He wants you. I think he's in love with you."

Jackson didn't comment. It was just too bizarre.

"You need to answer honestly, Jackson. Jack wants to know. Please, answer honestly. I don't want him to hurt Blake, and Jack will if you lie."

"Okay. Go ahead."

"Do you love Blake? Remember, Jack knows the answer, and if you lie to me, he'll kill him right here and now."

"Yes," Jackson hissed into the phone. "Yes, I love him, or at least, I think I might be falling in love with him. We haven't known each other too long, and it's early. Jack? Jack?"

"It's okay, Jackson, so far, so good. And it's Colin. Jack is gone for now, but he'll be back."

"You killed Tyler. How did it happen? Did Manny know about it? Was Manny there?"

"Jack killed Tyler. Not me. Manny left us with him. Tyler was pretty battered. Manny beat the crap out of him. He had to. Still, Tyler said he loved you. You never even laid a hand on him, and he still loved you. I tended his wounds. Daddy asked me to stay with him. I tried to kiss him, told him you were there, too. He didn't believe Jack was really you. He has never quite gotten that policeman swagger thing you have. It's sexy but hard to master. Don't tell Jack I told you, okay?" He was giggling.

Tears stung Jackson's eyes. His head was spinning. "Stop laughing. Listen. What did Manny do when he found out what you did, what Jack did to Tyler?"

"He was upset because Tyler was a good earner, but he wasn't going to turn me in. After all, Tyler was half dead anyway before I gave him what he wanted. Tyler was so silent. I tried to wake him. He was like an angel, so still."

"Did Manny help you take care of the body?"

"Yes. Tyler was heavy."

Jackson tried to keep his voice steady. "I'm at Trenton. Where do I go now? All I see are trees. Tell me where you are."

"Help me, Jackson. Jack is trying to silence me. I want to save Blake."

"Colin, hang on, fight him. I'll be there soon, I'll help you. I will save you this time."

"I have your picture, the one Tyler took of you together at the football game. I had it printed from his phone. I sleep with it. All those months that I was locked in the basement, the picture was all I had. When Jack would come, it kept the nightmares away. Even Jack likes that picture. He grew the shadow on his jaw, made his hair dark, just so he could look more like you."

*Good God.* "Basement? Manny locked you away in a basement after Tyler died?"

Whimpering. "It was dark. I was scared down there. Jack would come and hurt me."

"Colin, I can help you, protect you from Jack. Don't let him win."

He sobbed. "No, he's too strong, Jackson."

"Tell me where you are."

"I can't. He'll kill me. I have to wait. I'll ruin the game. He will bring you here in his own time."

"I won't let him kill you. I promise. Trust me, Colin. I won't let Jack hurt you anymore."

"The cabin," he whispered, "border crossing, green sign," he whispered.

Screaming.

"Colin? Colin? Is that Blake screaming?"

The line went dead. "Shit!" He dialed April.

She picked up right away. "Jackson? You all right?"

"Yeah, listen, a cabin, find out about a cabin at the border, I think he means the Philadelphia border, something about a green sign. Call me when you have anything. I'm almost there, another twenty minutes." He hung up and put the pedal to the floor.

The sun had gone down now. It was after seven in the evening, and Jackson was trying not to let the panic set in. Colin was definitely psychotic. Although Manny had beaten Tyler half to death, Colin had finished him. It must have given him a taste for murder. Manny realized that his son was sick, and rather than getting him the help he needed, that son of bitch had made it worse by locking him up in some dark basement. Now Colin's ego believed that he was *Jackson*? It was just too bizarre.

Jackson was at the border. He couldn't find any damn green sign. Maybe it was hidden by something. The snow had melted a lot, but there were still piles of it here and there in the fields.

The phone rang again. "Yeah?"

"We got a location," April told him. "Manny says there is a cabin, a few miles from New York, Phili border. There is a road, on the left, just as you pass the crossroads of Crescent and Yale. The road is called Ripple Road. There is a lake right at the end of it."

Jackson punched Crescent and Yale into his GPS. "Got it. Notify the others, but tell them to wait to move in. If Colin thinks I've brought the police, he could kill Blake before I get there. We are dealing with a very sick individual, two personalities, maybe more."

"Okay," April replied. "I hear you, buddy. Everyone is ready. Waiting for your call." She hung up.

Ten minutes later, Jackson passed Crescent and Yale. He slowed down, carefully checking for a road. He passed it three times before he realized where it was. The road was snowed in, the green sign half covered with sleet. *Shit*. He'd have to walk. And it had started to snow, just tiny flecks of it, but it could get worse.

Jackson pulled his vehicle over to the side of the road and locked it. He really could have used a pair of snowshoes. He had no idea how far this road went or how long it would take to get to the cabin. He buttoned up his coat and regretted not bringing gloves or a hat. The wind was howling around him. It was cold.

Walking wasn't easy. Due to the coming of spring, some of the patches in the road were soft, and Jackson sank to his knees a few times. He got up and kept going, his gaze scanning the trees and the road ahead, searching for any sign of a cabin. Chimney fire, lights?

He had been walking almost twenty minutes, and his hands were almost frozen. He could no longer feel his ears. He was tempted to call April and ask her if she knew how far this damn road went when he saw something out of the corner of his eye. He ran, stumbling a few times, sinking once, then getting up again and pressing on. Finally, there was a clearing.

The cabin was small, made of stone. There was one light burning in the window but no chimney fire. He had the advantage now. Colin wouldn't know he'd found him yet. Jackson took out his phone. The signal was there but weak. The trees were blocking it. Jackson put the phone back into his pocket and surveyed his surroundings, hoping the signal would be stronger in the clearing.

There was a car outside in front, a SUV minivan, and a road, partially cleared of snow, with fresh tracks. He couldn't take that road. Colin would see him. He'd have to go through the field and around back by the trees.

Jackson pressed on. The going was slow. His feet kept on sinking every few steps, forcing him to crawl out of his trap and forge forward again. He thought he'd never make it. When the phone rang, he was over halfway. He switched the phone to vibrate. It said Unknown Caller. It was him. Thankfully, the signal was back.

"Hello, Jackson."

The reception wasn't good, but he could hear him. "Who am I speaking to now, Colin or Jack?"

"Colin is hiding in his hole again."

Jackson closed his eyes. Damn. He was hoping he'd be Colin. "I see. You like to terrorize him."

He laughed. "Easy target. He's not like us."

"I'm nothing like you. So, are you going to tell me where you are?" Jackson took a few more steps.

Someone walked in front of the window.

"There's a road," he said. "It's called Ripple Road. Find it and you find me."

"I want to talk to Blake first." The phone was crackling.

"Why?"

"I want to know he's all right. If you've done something to Blake, hurt him in any way, I'm not coming. I told you that."

"That's it. That's my boy. The white knight. Wait. I'll let you talk to your prince."

Jackson took a few more steps. He was on solid ground now. He headed to a tree then trudged through a path that led around the back of the cabin, phone to his ear. He was beyond freezing now, his feet and clothes soaking.

"Jackson." It was Blake.

"Are you all right?"

"Yes. He's going to kill you. Don't, please, I—"

That was it.

Jack was back on the line. "Your prince is alive, and if you find me in the next half hour, I will let him go. Otherwise, I will put him in the lake with the others."

"Others?" Jackson said, coming to a halt. "How many others, Jack?"

"I'll tell you about all of them when you get here. We'll have a drink together."

"I know about your drinks. I think I'll pass."

He laughed.

"Jack, listen—"

The line went dead. Had he hung up, or was it the signal? Jackson looked at the phone. No, there was still a signal. He'd hung up.

Shit. How many has he killed and put in the lake?

Jackson dialed April. "Listen, I'm at the cabin. I'm ready to go in. Wait for my call. If you don't get one in a half hour, move in. The signal is not secure out here. He says there are others in the lake."

"Good God. How many?"

"I don't know. I'll try and find out what I can. The stolen vehicle is a SUV minivan."

"Yes, we're just getting it."

"The owner?"

"Missing."

"Shit."

"Okay, give me a half hour, then call for backup."

"Half hour? You got twenty minutes," she told him. "Be careful, Jackson."

During times like this when he knew he was going into a dangerous situation, all his training as a police officer kicked in to automatic. He pushed the fear away, the emotions. He wasn't religious so he didn't pray, but he did promise something or someone that if he got Blake out of this in one piece, he'd try and be a better man, stop drinking so much, leave the past behind.

There was only one door in the front, and the window in the back was a single pane. It must have been the bedroom window. Couldn't open it from the outside. Smashing it would make too much noise as there was more than three rooms in that cabin. Jackson moved around the side of the house, gun ready, trying to forget how cold and wet he was. There was another window beside the door, a very small one, not big enough for a child to get through. He carefully took a quick look inside. No movement or sound. There was a sofa, and beyond that, a small kitchen area. There was a fireplace but no fire burning. Jackson reached for the door handle. The door blew open as soon as he touched it. Jackson jumped back, staying close to the wall as the door banged over and over against the inside wall.

Jackson waited, breathing hard. So much for the advantage of surprise.

"Come in, Officer Blue," a voice welcomed. "You're early."

Jackson slowly walked in, his gun drawn. He could see Blake on the left side of the room in the corner. He was tied to a chair. Directly behind him stood Colin—or was it Jack?—a knife positioned at Blake's throat. He'd dyed his hair, had kind of a beard, looked fake. He was wearing sunglasses, strange. Then Jackson realized that they were his sunglasses. He must have left them at Blake's house that time.

"I suggest you put down the gun, Sergeant," he said. "You see, they make me nervous, something I have to master, being on the force. My hand gets shaky." He pressed the blade to Blake's throat to make his point.

Blake's gaze was on him. There was fear in his eyes.

Jackson put his gun on the small table just behind him.

"Oh no," Colin said, shaking his head. "That's too close. Jackson, really, we've both had training. Put your gun over there," he pointed, "in the bottom of the umbrella stand."

Jackson walked over and did as Jack told him. "Now, let

him go," Jackson said, turning to meet his gaze. "You can have me instead."

Colin moved the knife away from Blake's throat. Something shiny hung round his neck. A badge?

"Where did you get that?" Jackson asked, pointing to the badge.

"When I graduated academy. That's a strange question." He laughed.

"Is it real? Did you take it off a cop? Yes, that police officer you murdered in cold blood at my house."

"That was unfortunate," he said softly.

"Yes. Damn unfortunate. We don't kill our own, Jack."

"I know. I didn't have a choice. He was dirty, on the take, like a lot of the cops who used to handle Manny's whores. Blake can tell you stories. Right, Blake?" He poked him.

Blake nodded.

"Keep your word, Jack. Let him go. You can have me."

"No," Blake said, tears rolling down his face. "He'll kill you. He wants to be you. He wants to—"

Colin placed a hand on Blake's mouth, shook his head. "Quiet now. This is police business. I will say, it's very touching," he commented. "Could be the movie of the week, a real tear-jerker."

"Cut the crap," Jackson snapped, losing patience. "You want me? You want to pay me back for Tyler? Then take me, you coward, and let Blake go."

"You come here, surrender to me." Colin licked his lips. "The things I could do to you. You and I together."

"Untie him, let him go," Jackson said, meeting his gaze, moving closer.

Colin reached over and took a pair of handcuffs out of the drawer. He tossed them at Jackson. Jackson caught them in one hand. "Take off your clothes and put on the cuffs."

Blake was shaking his head. "No, Jackson."

"Let him go first," Jackson said, examining the handcuffs. They were regulation, police issue. He was sure they, too, had belonged to Officer Nivens. That meant Colin also had Niven's revolver.

"Take them off," Colin demanded. "Or I'll kill him, slit his throat like I did that kid cop."

"Release Blake."

"Even if I did, I'd only pick him up again later. He has no way out of here. He'd freeze."

Jackson shrugged. "Let him take his chances. Let him go, and you can have me."

"You are a fool, Jackson," he said, laughing as he reached down behind Blake. "You must have slept through the academy."

Jackson didn't comment. He waited. He had to get Blake out of harm's way before Colin heard the police sirens and the helicopter that would soon be overhead. Jackson took off the jacket. He met Blake's gaze, trying to reassure him.

"Your badge," Colin insisted, "give it to me." He held out his hand.

Jackson came closer, took off his badge. He handed it to him. It wasn't the real one anyway.

Blake was free, on his feet. A little unstable, he took a few steps toward Jackson.

Jackson reached out to steady him, pushing his coat at him. "Put my coat on and get out of here. Now." He knew the police would be here any minute but he couldn't tell Blake that.

"No, Jackson. I won't leave you." Blake clung to him. "I'll die out there anyway. I'd rather it be—"

"There's nothing between us, Blake." He gave him a little shove away. "We had some fun. It's over. Now go on."

The pain in Blake's face was clearly visible.

"Go!"

Blake shrugged into Jackson's jacket on the way to the door. He heard the door open and close. Jackson turned away.

"You are one cold bastard, Jackson." Colin smiled. "I've always been right about you."

Jackson sighed. "Right. So, we deserve each other."

"I stuck to my part of the bargain." Jack pointed at him. "Now, you keep yours."

"Why should I?" Jackson asked, dropping the handcuffs on the floor. "You should know better. I lied to Tyler to get information. I lied to Blake, too. So why in hell would I tell you the truth?"

"We're the same. I'm you, Jackson."

"No, you're not me, Jack," Jackson told him, coming closer. "You may want to be me, but you never will be. Do you want to know what you are? Do you want to know why Tyler and Blake never wanted you?"

Colin was becoming enraged. "It's not true. I'm you. My name is Jack. Jack. Jack." He was screaming. "I'm not Colin. Colin is dead." He looked at Jackson in disbelief. "You're a liar. I am you."

Jackson went to make a move then froze at a glint of steel in Colin's hand.

He raised his hand, pointing the gun at him. "I know you must have called in the rest of your scumbag friends, Jackson," he said, "but we'll both be dead before they get here."

"Okay, but if we're both going to die here, Jack, at least tell me about the others in the lake. I think it's a lie that you killed anyone. You don't have the guts for that."

Colin began to name the young men he'd killed, two in New York before Manny had taken him to Italy. Three in Italy, and seven more since he'd come back. "I left out the unimportant ones." He shrugged, as if their lives were merely collateral damage. "The cop and two others."

"Hubert Fontaine, the guy you stole the Audi from?"

"Regret that one. The car didn't run well."

"The SUV outside?"

"You're a cop, do your homework." He smiled.

"Sorry, I'm a little preoccupied. Why don't you go ahead and tell me about the driver?" Jackson folded his arms across his chest.

"Woman, blonde, forties."

Jackson shook his head. "Is she still alive?"

"I doubt it. I bashed her skull in with an iron rod, rolled her body into the ditch a few miles back."

"Where is Fontaine's Audi, in the ditch with her?" Jackson eyed him.

"So smart, good-looking and smart. You got it all when they were handing it out," he said, smiling.

"Tried to make it look like an accident, did you? Only thing is, bashing the skull in might not quite click with a car accident at the coroner's."

"Doesn't matter," he said. "This ends here, you and I."

"Why? Your father is the one who deserves to be punished, don't you think?" Jackson watched his face.

The expression darkened. "Colin loves him. He's always going on about Daddy this and Daddy that. He even forgives him for locking us up in the dark."

"Why did he do that?"

"You know why." Colin gave Jackson a sinister smile. "He thought it would end with Tyler. I did him a favor, you see? That's when Manny discovered I was you. He started calling me Jack."

"And Jack took over. Who was he before, when he killed Tyler? Not Colin. Colin couldn't have done that."

"You were growing inside me, Jack. You're always with me. That's why we have to die together. You want this to end? It will end, but for Jack to die, you need to die. There's no other way."

Jackson inched closer.

"Now, enough wasting time. Take off your clothes and put on the handcuffs like you promised, Jackson," he said, pointing the gun directly at him. "Let the party begin."

# CHAPTER EIGHT

When Blake stepped out into the night and the door closed behind him, his emotions were in turmoil. He stood with his back against the door, unable to take another step. He was free. The terror Colin had visited on him had left him paralyzed by fear. But he had a new fear now. Jackson. And this fear was nothing compared to what he'd felt for himself. He wouldn't leave him in there with that monster. He had to help him somehow, even if it meant he'd never get out of these woods alive. The hurtful words Jackson had told him inside were completely insignificant now. If something happened to Jackson, he wasn't sure how he'd go on. Did he love him? Damn it. He didn't want to think about love, but he knew one thing, he wasn't going to just walk off down that road knowing that Colin, Jack, or whoever he decided to be, was torturing Jackson.

When Blake heard the loud noise inside, he stiffened. There was breaking class and a gunshot. Blake ceased to think. Hyperventilating, he pushed open the door and ran inside. Jackson and Colin were struggling on the floor. There was blood. God, who was shot? Whose blood was that? Blake remembered that Colin had made Jackson put his gun in the umbrella stand. Blake grabbed it and tipped it over, retrieving Jackson's revolver. When he had it in his hand, he took off the safety, raised it to the ceiling, and pulled the trigger.

Plaster and pieces of ceiling came raining down around him as the two men suddenly lay silent on the floor. Blake approached and pointed the gun directly at Colin. Blake swallowed, glancing at Jackson who lay silently on his side. The knife, covered in blood, rested a few inches away.

"Jackson," Blake breathed, pausing at the sound of sirens in the distance.

Colin sat up. "How heroic, Blake. You must really love him to risk your life like that."

Blake wanted to go to Jackson, but he didn't dare move, his hand staying near the trigger of Jackson's gun. "I will shoot you, Colin. Get away from him, now." Blake choked back tears. He couldn't be dead.

The cops would be here soon. The sirens grew louder.

Colin reached his hand forward toward the knife.

"No," Blake cried out, racing forward. "I will shoot you. Jackson?"

Colin had the knife in his hand.

Jackson moaned and stirred.

Blake wanted to cry. He was alive. "Jackson, are you all right? I thought you were dead."

"I told you to get away from here," he muttered, struggling into a sitting position. He looked at Colin and staggered to his feet. "Put the knife down, Colin."

Jackson reached out his hand for his gun.

Blake handed it to him.

"Give me the knife, Colin. It's not worth it. Come on," Jackson urged.

"I'm not Colin," he said softly. "I'm Jack, and there's only room for one of us." With that, he raised the knife and slashed it across his own throat.

Blake covered his mouth and took a step back.

"Shit," Jackson cried out, taking off his t-shirt. He ripped it in two, trying to stop some of the bleeding. Colin was gurgling blood, losing far too much. Seconds later, he lay quiet. Jackson lifted his wrist, took his pulse. "He's gone," he said, almost to himself.

Blake was crying.

Jackson put his t-shirt over Colin's face and got to his feet, covered in blood. He took a step toward him but froze when the squeal of tires then the slamming of car doors rent the air. "You all right?" he asked him.

Blake gulped some tears. "I guess."

"Good, give me my phone. It's in the pocket of my coat."

"You left me your phone?" Blake reached in and took it out, handing it over. "You weren't sure you were coming out alive, were you?"

Jackson didn't answer. He opened his phone and pressed speed dial for April. "It's okay," he said. "Suspect is dead. Come on in." He hung up. He went to sit on the sofa.

"Jackson?" Blake came and sat beside him. "You're bleeding more than you think."

Jackson leaned back on the sofa. "I'm fine," he said softly and, reaching out his arm, he placed it around Blake's shoulders. "I'm sorry, Blake," he said.

"For what?" Blake's eyes teared over. "You saved my life."

"Sorry for everything," he breathed. Then his eyes closed.

"Jackson?" Blake said as Jackson's head lolled to the side.

The door opened. The police crowded in.

"April?" Blake cried as soon as she came in.

Her gaze settled on Jackson.

"He's bleeding a lot. I think he's unconscious."

April leaned closer to her partner, checking Jackson's eyes, his pulse. "Hey," she called out. "Someone. Help me over here." There was fear in her eyes. "We're going to lose him."

A couple of hours later, Blake paced around the stretcher in the emergency ward, waiting for the doctor to come back with his blood test results. He had some superficial cuts on his throat where Colin had scraped the blade over his skin but never really cut him. He was pretty sure the drug was out of his system now, but the doctors wanted to be sure. The nurse had dabbed something on his throat a while back, and it burned like hell.

No one told him anything about Jackson. April had only said that they were giving him a blood transfusion in the back of the ambulance. He was breathing but weak. They were going to do tests to see if there was any internal bleeding.

The doctor finally returned, a file in his hand. "Well, Mr. Wellington, there are still some traces in your bloodstream of Rohypnol but very little. Try to drink a lot, and it will come out in the urine. You're free to go, but there is a Detective Grant who wants you to check in with her before you leave."

"Okay, where is she?" Blake asked.

"On third floor, intensive care."

"Jackson," Blake breathed. "Do you know how he is? Detective Jackson Blue?"

"Sorry, no. You'll have to ask upstairs."

Blake ran down the hallway. Intensive care? What did that mean? He took the elevator to the third floor, only to be met by a sea of cops, in and out of uniform.

When April saw Blake, she walked down the hallway to meet him. "Are you all right?" she asked him.

"Yes, yes, never mind me. Jackson?" He held his breath. "How is Jackson?"

"He's lost a lot of blood," she said. "He had multiple stab wounds, one of them nicked an artery. He was bleeding internally. They found the bleed, and the hemorrhaging has stopped. They're keeping him overnight for observation. He should be fine. They'll move him to a ward tomorrow, and he'll be wanting to leave, knowing Jackson."

Blake blindly groped for a seat and lowered himself into one. He put his face in his hands.

April touched his shoulder. She sat beside him. "You really care about Jackson, don't you?"

He nodded silently then looked at her. "What happens now?" He wiped the tears from his eyes. He was exhausted in so many ways.

"You'll need to give a statement. Colin is dead, so you won't have a lengthy trail to sit through."

"What about Manny?" he asked.

"Manny is being charged with accessory to murder. He's being booked as we speak."

"Good," Blake said.

"What are you going to do now?" April Grant asked him.

"I don't know," he said. "I really don't know."

"I'm sure Jackson would be all right with you staying with him. Only his place is still a crime scene, and I don't know if—" April paused. "So, do you have any money?"

"A bit." He told her. "Enough to see me through a month or two."

"Come and stay with me tonight, okay?" She smiled at him. "We'll figure something out in the morning."

"Thanks. That's really kind of you, but I want to stay here with Jackson."

"You're exhausted, Blake. Are you sure? You want me to see if we can get you a cot somewhere then?"

"No. I won't sleep. I don't want to cry," he told her. "But damn it, I think I may love that man. And I can't be doing that, loving him." He shook his head.

"Why not?" she asked. "You think you don't deserve love?"

"Not his love, I don't. We are so different. I have nothing to offer him."

"How about you? You could offer him you."

Blake wiped his eyes, tearing up again. "That wouldn't be enough."

"Why not let Jackson be the judge of that?"

"No. He'll end up looking after me. I need something of my own. Can you help me with that?"

"Find a job, you mean?"

"I want to go to university. I finished my high school. I have good marks. I just don't know how to go about it."

"I'd be glad to help you," she said. "But Jackson would help you, too. I know he would."

He met her gaze. "No. I want to do this for myself, and for him. I just didn't know leaving him would hurt this much." Blake lowered his head, and the tears flowed.

April stroked his hair. "Love hurts, but it's always worth fighting for. What do you want to do?"

"Jackson deserves a man, a man worthy of how wonderful he is. I want to help kids on the street."

"Social work maybe?" April lifted an eyebrow.

"Yeah. I could get a loan, a part-time job. My marks were good in high school. I found out I'm pretty smart." He smiled.

April hugged him. "What are you going to tell Jackson?"

"Nothing for now. I think I need to do this alone. If he knows, he'll try to help me too much. It's in his nature. I have to try and stand on my own two feet."

"What if you lose him?" April met his eyes. "What if during all that, someone else comes along, and he falls in love with him? He's going to think you abandoned him."

"I'll have to take that chance." He sighed. "I need to show him what kind of man I could be when I go to him. Then I'll tell him how I feel but I'll have something to give him then, something we can build a future on. I might even propose." He grinned.

"Good heavens." April laughed. "That I'd like to see, Jackson in a tux."

Blake squeezed April's arm. "Me, too," he said.

Blake was convinced that he was doing the right thing. It seemed April, however, wasn't. She helped Blake fill out forms and directed him to where he needed to go, even helped him find a job, but the entire time she told him she felt guilty. "I'm lying to him," she said. "I'm lying to my partner."

The last time Blake saw Jackson, he'd been sitting up in a bed complaining about being kept in the hospital. That adorable patch of hair was in his eyes, and he seemed genuinely happy to see him.

"Do you need a place a stay?" Jackson had asked him. "Until you get on your feet you can stay with me. My apartment should be habitable soon. I think I should move, don't you?"

"I would if I were you," Blake said, hovering near the door. "Don't worry about me, though. I'll be fine." He didn't want to get too close to the bed. He didn't want to touch him or kiss him, because then he'd never walk away. "I have plans."

"Oh, okay," Jackson said. "Something I can help you with?"

Blake smiled. "No."

"So, what then?" Jackson met Blake's gaze. "This is it? Goodbye? We've been through a lot together. I thought we'd stay friends, at least."

Jackson was breaking his heart, and the look on his face was confusion mixed with disappointment. Blake made an attempt to change the subject. "How do you feel?"

"Okay. My gut hurts a bit, but other than that, I'm fine. They operated by laser, so it won't leave a scar, and the recovery is quick. Luckily the wounds were superficial."

"So, back to work soon."

"I've got some time off coming. Think I'll take two weeks." He met Blake's gaze. "Blake?"

Blake bit his bottom lip. "What?" His voice came out like a whisper. He looked at the floor.

"What I said to you at the cabin, when I was trying to get you to leave, I didn't mean any of that. I had to say it because—"

Blake put up a hand. "It's okay, Jackson. Let's not go there, okay?"

"If I hurt you, I didn't mean to. I was only trying to get you out of harm's way before—"

"I realize that. Thank you for saving my life."

"Thanks for saving mine," he said.

Blake smiled. "Get well, okay?" He turned and practically ran from the room.

Jackson called his name.

He stayed at April's for a week until she found him a good job in a warehouse at night. He applied for his loan and rented a room in an apartment with two other guys. They were university students. Blake hoped to start the following term. He got his loan and an interview to the social work program.

When he was busy, he didn't think about Jackson. But when the night came, and he crawled under the covers, he ached for him. April kept him abreast of things. Jackson was working hard. They'd been out a few times, and some guys chatted Jackson up, but nothing had developed.

"Are you sure?" Blake asked her over coffee one evening at a little café near the university. "Has he been taking men home, sleeping with someone?"

"He hasn't mentioned anyone. And I don't know everything he does. He's got a new place, nice. And he is in line for a promotion."

"Oh yeah?" Blake smiled. "He's so smart, a great cop."

"Caused some problems between us for a while. I have seniority, but the serial killer case pushed his promotion ahead of mine."

"Sorry."

"No, it's okay. Now I'm up for it, too. Jackson is helping me study for it. He's an angel."

Blake grinned. "I wouldn't call Jackson an angel. He's beautiful and a good cop."

"You've got it bad, boy." She threw a napkin at him. "First semester is over. Going to get a second job this summer?"

"No, I'm taking the summer session," he said. "But I have a chance to do some street work at a walk-in center. If I get it, it will count toward my work placement. It's perfect—they deal with a lot of teenage runaways."

"I'm so proud of you," April said, touching his hand. "I wish you'd tell Jackson what you're doing. I know he misses you. I think you should get in touch with him, Blake. Enough now."

"Did he say he missed me?" Blake persisted. "Does he mention me?"

"Yes, I told you that. He said it the other day. He wondered what you were up to, if you were all right. He said he was going to look you up, and I told him not to do that." She sat back with a sigh. "I said probably you had moved on. But I can't put him off all the time, Blake. One of these days, he just might show up at your door." She eyed him. "He is a cop, he'll find you. What would you do then?"

Blake smiled. "Considering I haven't been laid for six months, I'd probably ravish him right there."

"You haven't had sex since Jackson?" April shook her head in disbelief.

"I don't want anyone but Jackson."

"Aw, sweetie, you're going to make me cry," April said. "Look, things are going well. Why not see him now? I know you want to. Just let him know what's happening. Leave the ball in his court."

Blake nodded, smiling. "All right. Give me his address and tell me when he'll be home, okay?"

April gave him a high five.

Blake was filled with *what-ifs?* as he got off the bus near Jackson's new apartment two days later. It was four in the afternoon. April assured him Jackson would be home and awake. He'd just come off the night shift.

Blake stood in the small park across from Jackson's building for a good twenty minutes before he got up the courage to ring the man's doorbell. He almost walked away a few times. He really didn't have any right to expect that Jackson would want him. It was a fantasy in his mind really, one April had encouraged. He had his life on track. That was something. He worried that if things didn't go his way today, it would derail him. No, he had to promise himself that no matter what happened with Jackson, he would keep on going, become a social worker, try to do some good in this world.

Blake paused in front of the building, checking his reflection in the glass door. He'd put on some weight since he'd last seen Jackson. He wasn't dancing anymore, or tricking. It looked good on him. His hair was shorter, and he'd bought some nice pants and shirts. Today he'd chosen black pants and a navy shirt, open at the collar. He straightened his hair a few times before he pressed the apartment number with a shaking finger.

When he heard Jackson's voice, Blake closed his eyes. *I love you. I love you.* It was insane, but the sound of Jackson's voice made him feel weak inside. He placed his forehead against the wall.

"Hello? Yes?" Jackson said again.

"Jackson," Blake replied. "It's me. It's Blake."

Silence.

Blake waited. For a moment, he thought Jackson wasn't going to let him in, then the door buzzed open. Blake walked down the hall. He was perspiring. Jackson's apartment was on the ground floor. At the end of the hall was the man he loved more than anything, and it was a wild, scary feeling that had his heart hammering. He'd never known love, and now there was part of him that feared it. But he knew he didn't want to live without this big, bad cop he'd found, no matter what it took.

When Blake got to the door, Jackson was standing there in navy jogging pants and a white t-shirt with the NYPD emblem on it, that unruly dark hair of his endearingly messy and in his eyes.

Blake swallowed. "Hi."

Jackson met his gaze, his expression unreadable. "Ah, come in," he said, leaving the door open and walking down the hall.

Blake closed the door, following Jackson into the living room. "This is nice," he said. There were still boxes piled in the corner by the window. "Not all moved in, I see."

Jackson put some space between them. It was strained. Blake was regretting coming here.

"I have been working a lot lately. No time. Want a drink?" Jackson moved farther away, to the small kitchen. "I have ice tea."

"Yeah, okay," Blake replied, looking around. "How have you been?"

He came out with a glass of tea. He handed it to him. "Do you care?"

*Ouch.* "Of course, I care," Blake replied, taking the glass from him.

Jackson just shrugged. "I'm okay, I guess. I haven't heard from you in half a year. I thought you'd left the city."

"No."

"So . . . you must be doing pretty well then, nice clothes, put on twenty pounds about. Expensive restaurants every night? Your new patron must be a very rich man."

Blake put the glass on the coffee table. "Is that what you think, that I have some man buying me clothes, that I'm still in the trade? Well, I'm not surprised you'd think that," he said. "I'll be going now."

Damn it. Is this what a broken heart feels like? To hell with love then.

# CHAPTER NINE

Jackson stood riveted to the spot. Blake showing up at his door had really thrown him for a loop. What the hell was going on? He hadn't seen head nor tail of the guy for months, and now he just shows up, dressed fancy, obviously eating very well. What did he want him to think?

He went to the window, thinking he'd catch sight of Blake walking away. He was already gone. He'd left here as if his tail was on fire. "Damn it." He'd jumped to conclusions maybe. He could be wrong. And he had no right to judge him. It was just that . . . just that what? That he really did care, a little too much? That seeing him like that had his mouth going dry and his head spinning? "Blake," he said. When Blake had left his hospital room, Jackson had a feeling he wouldn't see him again. They both knew a relationship between them was impossible. They were great in bed together, but there had to be more for there to be a long-term commitment.

Jackson cracked open a beer and turned on the television. There was a hockey game on, teams he wasn't really into. He watched it with little interest, his mind on Blake. The whole idea of long-term commitment was a little off-putting. He'd been in one of those with Rob. It had ended badly. Now, to think about another with a guy with Blake's history? And why was he even thinking that? Maybe Blake had just wanted to say hello. After all, they'd shared a horrific experience, and they had been intimate. He should have been nice.

He finished the beer and told himself to forget it. He was

off tonight. Maybe he should go out and bring someone home. It was embarrassing to think that Blake was the last person he'd had sex with. It wasn't for lack of opportunity. He found himself making excuses. What if he brought home some weirdo who after one night wouldn't stop stalking him? Wasn't he getting too old for the bar scene? He'd expected his life to be different now. He thought he'd still be with Rob, or some other stable partner, who wanted to share a life with him, grow old with him. Instead he was alone, and scared to grow into some crusty old cop, who fed his goldfish after work, alone, asexual, ogling young men at intersections.

"Damn it!" He got to his feet. This was stupid. He was working himself into a frenzy, and all this because Blake had stopped by. He checked the time. It was after six. He'd take a shower, get dressed, and go to that little gay bar he liked for a drink. One drink, and maybe some conversation. Maybe more?

He had just gotten out of the shower when his buzzer rang. He wrapped the towel around his waist and snaked a hand through his wet hair. "Blake?" The name came instantly to his lips. He pressed the buzzer. "Listen, I'm sorry, please, come in, we'll talk."

"It's April," the voice said. And she sounded peeved about something.

He pressed the button, his heart sinking. When he opened the door, he said, "What are you doing here? It's our day off. I thought you'd be with Verity. Aren't you seeing her anymore?"

April walked in and closed the door. "She's working," she said, looking at him. "You're really buff now, Jackson, is working out compensating for lack of sex?"

"Shut up," he said.

"Are you going somewhere?"

"I was," he said. "It's Saturday night. I've got two days off."

"Going for a drink at The Current?"

"Maybe."

"I'll come with," she offered.

"No, you will not come with," Jackson told her. "I'd like to have some space without my partner slash surrogate girlfriend tagging along."

"Well, I need to talk to you," she said. "So, put some clothes on. You don't want to end up turning me straight or something."

"Yeah, right," Jackson said, leaving her in the living room. What was this about now? He didn't want to get into any deep conversations. They did that enough on the job together. Things had been a little rough since he'd made lieutenant. Technically he was now her superior, and really, she should have been promoted before him. He was doing all he could to help her, not that she needed any. He couldn't wait for her to make lieutenant so he could stop feeling like such a misogynistic prick.

Jackson put on a pair of tight-fitting jeans and a white muscle shirt. It was true he had put on some more muscle mass and heightened the definition. He spent a lot of his free time in the gym.

When he walked out, April whistled. "Okay, you're hot. Don't let it go to your head."

Jackson grinned. "Okay, what do you want?"

"A drink to start. You better have one, too."

"Why do I need a drink?" He eyed her.

"Just pour us one and stop being the interrogator for five minutes."

Jackson poured her some scotch in a glass and sat beside her.

"Where's yours?"

"I'm not drinking much anymore," he said.

"Really?" She smiled. "Good." She sipped her drink. "Are you intending to get laid tonight?"

"That's the idea."

"Don't."

"Why in the hell not?"

"You won't have a problem getting laid."

"But? April? What is it?" He leaned forward. "You're talking crazy. What do you care if I get laid or not?"

"What are you going to drink at the bar?"

"A light beer. Will you stop changing the subject. What is it that's got you all jittery?"

"Blake was here, wasn't he?"

Jackson took a step back. "How the hell do you know that?"

"I just do." She finished the drink, looked around the room. "Nice curtains."

"Forget the damn curtains. You've been in communication with Blake?" He was stunned. All the times he'd brought up the subject of Blake, and they'd speculated as to what had happened to him. She'd even dissuaded him from trying to track him down, more than once.

"Yes," she said, putting up a hand. "And I know what you're thinking."

"No, you damn well do not. You never told me you were in touch with him. Why didn't you tell me?"

"He didn't want me to."

He nodded, his heart sinking. "Why did he come here now then? To tell me about his new boyfriend?"

"It's not what you think, Jackson. It's not because he didn't want to see you. And there is no one else."

"What then?"

"You hurt him deeply. He's not hustling anymore. There's no sugar daddy supporting him. Why do you always have to be like that?"

"Like what?"

"A prick, who assumes the worse in people."

"I'm a cop. That's what we do, April. Given his history, what did he expect me to believe when he shows up here like that?"

"You might have given him the benefit of the doubt, given him a chance to explain before you jumped all over him."

"You seem to know a lot about Blake. Just how long have you guys been hanging out?" He stood, crossing his arms over his chest.

"I've been helping him."

"Helping him do what exactly?"

"He loves you, Jackson. He wants to be with you but —"

"Bullshit. If he'd wanted to be with me, he wouldn't have disappeared. Not a word, not a call. Nothing. I thought he'd . . . forgotten all about me." There, he'd said it. The hurt was in clear view. "He just wrote me off."

"He made a mistake. He realizes that now, but he did it for a good reason. He's gone back to school. He got a loan and a job. He's going to be a social worker. He wanted to come to you as a man, with a future, something to offer you. Jackson, he wants to marry you." Tears rolled down April's cheeks.

Jackson's eyes widened. He plunked down on the sofa. "He wants to *what*?"

"He wants to propose. He had it all worked out. I told him not to wait, to tell you now. I was worried you'd find someone else in the meantime."

Jackson closed his eyes. "Oh God." He rubbed his eyes. "Propose?"

"Yes, he's mental, wanting to marry you."

Jackson made a face.

"He was crying when he called me. We both decided

you're a big brute and mean as hell."

"Thanks."

"I don't want him to give up on what he's accomplished so far. He's been in counselling to deal with his past, but without you, he'll fail. I know it."

"Where is he?" Jackson asked her.

April smiled, jumped to her feet. She pulled him up with her. "I'll take you to him."

Jackson shook his head. "No, I'll go on my own."

"You belong together, Jackson. He's done all this for you."

"Okay," he said. "I believe you. You don't have to take me. Just give me the address."

Jackson threw on his leather jacket and walked with April outside. Autumn leaves were scattered across the parking lot, and it had already gotten dark. Jackson watched April drive away, still not sure how he felt about her lying to him. Blake was no more than a twenty-minute car ride away. So close and yet so far. If he'd only known.

The apartment building where Blake lived was a short walk from the university. Jackson parked across the street. It was a nice building, four apartments, each with a separate balcony, with a well-maintained lawn. He stood at the main entrance for a few minutes, unsure of himself. What was he going to say?

A man came out, and Jackson grabbed the door and walked into the lobby. The floors were clean, no graffiti on the walls. Jackson checked the mailboxes and found one with three names, one of which was B. Wellington. Apartment Three. It was on the second floor.

Jackson walked up the stairs. He hesitated at the top then forced his feet to move forward. In front of apartment three, he paused then knocked.

A young man answered, a handsome-looking African

American in his twenties. He smiled at him, giving him the once-over. "Hello there. Well, it's not my birthday, so what can I help you with?"

Jackson smiled. "I'm looking for Blake. Is he here?"

"Lucky, Blake," he said. "Yeah, he's in his room. Want me to call him?"

"No, I'll, ah, just go in if you don't mind."

"You must be Jackson," he said, as if it suddenly dawned on him. "Um, no wonder Blake is holding out."

Jackson walked past him. "Which way?" he asked.

"At the end of the hallway, beside the bathroom. I'll just be out here if something doesn't pan out for you."

Jackson looked at him, smiled, but didn't comment. Instead, he knocked at Blake's bedroom door and turned the handle.

Blake was on the bed. He shot up into a sitting position when he saw Jackson walk in and close the door.

"So, I'm a big brute, am I?" Jackson said, leaning back against the closed door. "Not to mention mean."

Blake lifted his legs over the side of the bed. "What are you doing here? How did you find me?"

"Why didn't you tell me, Blake? I could have helped you. I would have, you know that."

Blake glanced down at his folded hands. "I wanted to do it for you, on my own."

Jackson moved forward. He went down on his haunches in front of him. "But we could do it together," he said, lifting Blake's chin with his fingers. "That's what people do when they love each other."

Blake's eyes widened. He met his gaze. "Did you say . . . love?"

"Yes, and I'm sorry. I was just so surprised at seeing you again. I thought you'd abandoned me."

"Abandoned you?" Blake whispered. "I love you, Jackson. I think I fell in love with you the first night we met."

"With my homeless get-up on?" Jackson raised an eyebrow. "You are a big, fat liar, Blake Wellington."

"Well, maybe after you came out of the shower." Blake grinned.

Jackson chuckled. He went to sit beside him on the bed. "Do you think we are impossible, Blake?"

Black swallowed. "It doesn't feel that way with you this close to me. I want you so much."

"Me, too," Jackson said, leaning in close and pressing his mouth to his in a tender kiss. He pulled back again while he had the strength. "You need to promise me that you won't keep anything from me again. If we are going give this relationship a go, I need to be able to trust you."

"Give this . . . ah . . . relationship a go?" Blake stuttered out Jackson's statement. "Did you just say that?"

Jackson nodded. "It won't be easy. My job is crazy. You will have to learn to live with a cop, but if you can do that, not to mention that the general consensus is that I'm mean and nasty, possibly even a bastard."

Blake grinned. "You're not so bad."

"Gee, thanks," Jackson laughed. "Listen," he sobered, "I promise to love you for as long as you want me to, in sickness and health, and all that jazz."

Blake's eyes filled with tears. "I want to marry you."

"I know," Jackson said softly, touching his cheek. "April told me."

"Don't be mad at her." Blake took his hand. "She only did what I asked her to. Finally, I realized that being without you wasn't worth it."

"I would have accepted you as you were, the stripper, the hustler, although I would have hated the thought of sharing you with another man." Jackson made a face. "But the thought of being without you completely would have been worse than all that."

"The only man I want to strip for is you," Blake said softly.

"That's reassuring, and I'd take you up on that offer if your roommate wasn't listening at the door." Jackson grinned.

Jackson jumped off the bed and tore the door open. There he was.

"Oh, hi," the roommate said, gazing at Jackson. "Need a hand?"

"Roger, get lost," Blake told him. "Please?"

Roger slapped Blake on the arm. "Okay. I'll go for a bike ride, but you owe me." He winked at Jackson. "Damn, that's one fine man. You owe me a whole, big lot. Are you sure I can't—"

"Okay." Blake gave him a push. "Goodbye." He closed his door.

Jackson unzipped his coat and took it off.

"Wow," Blake said, coming closer, running his hand over Jackson's biceps. "Been working out a lot?"

"April says it's compensation for sex," Jackson said, pulling off Blake's t-shirt. "I haven't had any since you."

Blake's eyes widened. "Really? Seriously?" He smiled.

"What are you smiling about?" Jackson grumbled good-naturedly. "It's no laughing matter. I could have forgotten how."

"I doubt that." Blake kissed his neck. He unzipped Jackson's jeans. "Are your balls blue?"

"They might be," he said softly, taking Blake's face between his hands and kissing his mouth hotly.

"Um," Blake responded. "I can fix that for you."

"I know, I know," Jackson replied with a groan as Blake gave him a shove back on the bed.

Blake put his hands on both sides of Jackson's face. "So

damn beautiful, sexy. I want you, Sergeant Blue." Blake pulled off Jackson's boots then his jeans.

"Lieutenant Blue," he corrected with a grin and a clearing of his throat.

Blake straddled his hips and moved his palms over Jackson's chest and abs. "Yes, sir, and ah, so all lieutenants on the force come with these muscles, hard and defined?" Blake ran his hands over Jackson's biceps.

"I haven't investigated that scenario yet."

"Never mind." Blake shook his head. "Who you trying to impress? You're not going to be in one of those calendars, are you? Damn it." He licked Jackson's chest. "You could be the cover model."

Jackson responded by lifting Blake off him and rolling him over on the bed. He raised Blake's hands above his head and pressed him to the mattress. "You are gorgeous, you know that?" Jackson told him. "And now you're mine, all mine, and the only one I'm posing for is you, baby."

"I like the sound of that," Blake muttered, their mouths coming together again in sweet, hot kisses.

Jackson's cock was hard as hell. "Oh, damn it, Blake, I've missed you," he groaned against his mouth.

"I've missed you, too, baby." That was no lie.

"I can't wait to be inside you."

Blake's fist tightened around his shaft as Jackson finished undressing Blake. "These clothes off," he insisted.

"Um, I have to taste your big, juicy cock," Blake said. "I've missed it so much."

They rolled together on the bed until Jackson was under Blake. Blake snaked down, kissing Jackson everywhere, parting his thighs then licking the length of Jackson's shaft.

Jackson closed his eyes. Oh yes, he'd missed him. He'd missed his tongue and his mouth, and his hands touching his skin. But he'd missed other things, too—the way Blake looked at him when he wanted to fuck, the way he sighed, his stubborn streak that made everyone aware he wouldn't be pushed around. His Blake. And as Blake continued to swallow every inch of Jackson's cock, he knew they were meant to be. No matter what, they'd make it work somehow. This kind of love was worth it.

# You may also enjoy the following from eXtasy Books Inc:

*Borderline*
D.J. Manly

Excerpt

Summer: 2071

He filled the doorway like a shadow, a wide brimmed hat sitting low on his forehead. He seemed almost surreal as he placed a hand inside his trench coat and pulled out the package. I stared at it, nodding solemnly. "How do I know you don't have a copy somewhere?"

"There was only one, believe me."

I closed my eyes for a second.

"It was quite a read."

I didn't reply. I reached over and picked up a brown envelope off the coffee table.

"Is that the money?"

"Yes, it's what you asked for."

The man leaned down and placed the package at his feet.

I rose, placing my hand on the chair arm to propel myself into a standing position. I was suddenly feeling a little weak. This book meant everything to me. "Open the package.

Show it to me. I want to make sure it's my diary."

The young man bent over and picked it up. He ripped off the paper and held it up. There it was. It was mine alright. I recognized the red binding. That old brown elastic I had wound around it to keep it from falling apart was still there. "Hand the money over, and I'll pass it to you."

I held out the envelope. The man snatched it up and pushed the package hesitantly in my direction. I wrapped my hand around it, my breathing growing more rapid. When it was in my hands, I pressed it against my chest. My throat felt tight.

The man in the door tucked the envelope inside his coat. "Well, it's been a pleasure doing business with you."

"Get out of my house."

He paused, his eyes narrowing. "So, before I leave, are you going to tell me how it ended, or has it ended? You got right to the part . . . well, you never finished. Did you ever see him again?"

"That's none of your business."

"Ha," he scoffed, "you Hampton's. You're all the same. You use people and then throw them away."

I held my breath. I walked back to my chair, grateful to be sitting down again. I ran a hand over the faded red cover, then lifted it and pressed it to my chest again. There was a time when I was sure it was lost to me forever. The tears threatened for real now. I pushed them back, swallowed hard, and carefully pulled the elastic off. It fell open in my hands, the pages a little brown around the sides. I stared at the first page . . . July 12th, 2042 . . . twenty five years ago. I was barely twenty and about to get married . . .

I got up, and walked to the door. The man was just about to get into his car. I walked onto the porch and called to him. "Wait."

July 12, 2042

The hammers were ringing outside my bedroom window. They had started early that morning. They were setting up the tent and building the arch for the wedding. "God," I cried out, pulling the pillow over my head. They were giving me the worse headache. "Argggggggg!" I threw the pillow across the room and crawled out of bed, heading to the bathroom. "It's only eight o'clock for fuck's sakes. What's the rush? The wedding isn't for two weeks and . . . arggggg! I can't stand this anymore."

"Dominic," my mother opened the bedroom door suddenly and pocked her head in, "what are you screaming about? We can hear you all the way downstairs."

"Mother, God damn it, a little privacy please. I'm trying to take a piss."

Mother walked into the room and waited patiently until I came out of the bathroom. "Now, what's all the fuss?"

"Do they have to do that now at this time of morning?"

"Darling, you know your father doesn't trust the outsiders, and he wanted to be here to supervise the work. We don't have a lot of time. We are going to visit your grandmother tomorrow and . . ."

I sank down on the edge of the bed, running a weary hand through my golden blond hair. "I'm not going."

"Not going where?"

"To Grandmother's. I want some peace. I just finished the law exam from hell, and I'm exhausted. I want some time to myself before the wedding."

"Grandmother will be disappointed."

"Well, she'll see me at the wedding."

"What are you going to do in this big house all alone for a

week?"

"Sleep," I suggested with a smile.

My mother laughed lightly, coming over to smooth back some of my ruffled blond hair. "They'll be gone this afternoon. Come down and have some breakfast," she invited. "And you should call Vanessa. You haven't seen her in days."

"It's not good to see the bride before the wedding."

"Well, not in her dress but . . ."

"I'll call her, Mother."

"Well do it before she leaves to go to Europe to buy her trousseau."

"She's not leaving until day after tomorrow."

"Okay, get some clothes on and come downstairs," she said, clacking across the floor in her high heeled shoes.

I watched her leave, then stood up and walked over to the window. Below in the distance were Outsiders, three of them, working on my wedding arch. Male, two middle aged, one young with his shirt off, sweating, his hair plastered to his head. It was hard to see his face. Was he handsome? I ran my tongue unconsciously over my lips. I forced myself to move away. It didn't matter if he was handsome. I had no right to think that, no right to care. I moved away from the window, threw on a robe and headed downstairs.

# ABOUT THE AUTHOR

I write not only for my own pleasure, but for the pleasure of my readers. I can't remember a time in my life when I haven't written and told stories. When I'm not writing, I'm dreaming about writing, doing something wild and adventurous, or trying to make the world a better and more open minded place to live in. I adore beautiful men, and I know I'm not alone in this! Eroticism between consenting adults, in all its many forms is the icing on the cake of life!

D.J. has published well over two hundred novels/novella's, and is a well-seasoned writer.

www.ingramcontent.com/pod-product-compliance
Lightning Source LLC
Chambersburg PA
CBHW060823120626
46557CB00001B/349